Every Witch Way but Gone

Magical Misfits Mysteries - book 15

K.E. O'Connor

K.E. O'Connor Books

Chapter 1

Wedding day blues

"Juno! We can't delay for a second longer. I have other things to do. Much more important things." Cythera paced beside me, her white wings fluttering in a show of frustration and general grumpiness. It had been her default mood for weeks.

I chose not to respond as I stood at the back of the outdoor altar in the middle of Crimson Cove woods. My fur was groomed, my claws polished, and I'd attached a sparkly collar around my neck. But I was still missing something. Something that made me complete. My wonderful witch, Zandra Crypt, wasn't here, and her mother was about to get married. Zandra would never miss this special, magical day.

Cythera prodded me with the toe of her white boot. "Stop thinking about yourself. Zandra has been gone for weeks, and she's not coming back for this shambles."

"She'll be here. And this is Adrienne and Joel's special day, not a shambles." My gaze was fixed on the path leading away from the outdoor wedding venue. "They've had their differences, but Zandra would never forget her own mother's wedding."

Cythera snorted. "More than a few differences. And I've known Adrienne longer than you. She's always been wild. She's spoken about the things Zandra missed out on when she was younger, and they weren't small things. Some people can't forgive and forget. Your witch is one of them."

"Zandra and Adrienne have reconciled. And my witch doesn't hold grudges." Zandra sometimes did, but now wasn't the moment to point that out. "And she's a bridesmaid! The only bridesmaid, since everyone else was concerned about getting bitten if Adrienne got over-excited and forgot her manners. Zandra is also walking Adrienne along the aisle. She's a crucial part of this wedding."

"If you delay any longer, the ghouls will get hungry, and we don't want them eating the guests. Imagine the paperwork I'll have to complete."

"I made sure Adrienne and Joel had hearty meals before getting dressed," I said. "And they know to behave at such an important event. Besides, there are only a few of us here, and we all know how to handle ghouls if they get bitey."

Cythera checked her watch and sighed.

I glanced up at her, biting down on my anger. "Are we keeping you from something?"

"Yes! My job. I didn't want to be the wedding officiator."

Maverick, Cythera's rather wonderful husband, had convinced her to take on this duty. She'd complained bitterly for days afterward, but I thought we'd gotten past that. Apparently not.

"We'll delay for five more minutes," I said. "Adrienne will be so upset if Zandra doesn't show. I don't want to risk unsettling her, since she's already jittery from the pre-wedding nerves."

"This is a waste of time," Cythera grumbled as she set to pacing again.

I glanced over my shoulder at the small number of guests who were attending the wedding. We'd deliberately kept it to a select group. Sorcha Creer was a guest, along with Tia Starbow from the bakery, who'd made a special offal cake for after the ceremony. Cannibal Bill was also there – he'd become a great friend to Adrienne and Joel, giving them a place to stay and all the offcuts from his hunting they desired. So were Barney Hoffman and his familiar, Ember, from animal control. I'd invited Sage as my plus one, although it had been a challenge to force her out of bed, since she was morbidly depressed.

I was struggling not to join her in the misery fest. But I couldn't think about my problems. Not at this moment. Today was the happy couple's day, and as much as I wanted Zandra to be here to celebrate alongside us, it seemed she wasn't showing for her own mother's wedding.

I turned to the altar with a resigned sigh. "Let's get this thing started."

"At last!" Cythera threw up her hands then turned and stomped back to the small, leaf-entwined and flower-covered altar in front of the seating.

Joel waited there in a smart gray suit, shuffling from foot to foot and occasionally letting out a low groan. He was a quiet ghoul and always well-behaved whenever Adrienne was around. She was an excellent influence on him.

I trotted in the opposite direction from Cythera to collect Adrienne. She was dressed and ready to go, concealed behind a tree so Joel wouldn't see her outfit until she walked along the aisle. In Zandra's absence, I'd escort Adrienne and give her away. It was a privilege to do so.

I poked my head around the side of the tree. Adrienne's eyes widened a fraction, a hopeful glint in her hazy irises. "Zandra here?"

"I'm sorry. Something important must have delayed her. We both know she wanted to be here for you."

She sighed softly, a gray tinge to the fingers clutching her bouquet of daisies. "Zandra loves her work. A good girl. Must be that keeping her away."

"Zandra loves you, too. There'll be a reason she couldn't get back in time. But don't worry. Today is about you and Joel and making you the happiest couple in Crimson Cove. Shall we get you married?"

Adrienne adjusted one of the thin straps of her white, knee-length dress. It was pretty, simple, with a small amount of sparkle on the bodice. "I'm nervous. Should I get married?"

"Only if you want to. You do, don't you? It's not too late to change your mind." I hopped onto a fallen log and gazed up at her.

"Stomach feels funny. Bad offal?" She patted her stomach.

"Wedding jitters. I sniffed your food before you ate. There was nothing wrong with it."

"Jitters? Yes. Bad luck with past loves. Zandra's father included."

"But you learn and change." And Adrienne had changed. She was the only person I knew who'd improved by turning into a ghoul!

"Yes. Happy now. Love Joel."

"He loves you, too. And everyone is here to support you," I said. "Just look at Joel and smile. Then you'll know you're doing the right thing."

"I lost a tooth last week." Adrienne revealed a new gap in her smile.

"Joel will love you no matter how many teeth, toes, or fingers you lose. Shall I go ahead, and you can hold on to my tail?" It was a rare treat for anyone to touch my gorgeous tail, but Adrienne deserved to be indulged on her wedding day.

It took a few seconds of shuffling around before we got into a comfortable position, Adrienne lightly gripping the tip of my fluffy tail. Then we were off. The soft whisper of the wedding march drifted around us, and the guests stood. Adrienne shambled behind me, occasionally growling a greeting as we passed guests.

Her fingers tightened around my tail, but I didn't complain. She was nervous. But she squeezed so hard, it became painful. I looked back at Adrienne, and her lips were pulled back in an almost feral snarl.

Ghouls were difficult supernaturals to control. Most of them were ruled by their primal urge to hunt and destroy anything with a pulse. Adrienne had defied the odds by remaining stable. More stable than she'd been when she was a regular magic user. But heightened emotions interfered with her stability, and I sensed the tension and excitement of the day was getting to her. When ghouls lost control, they didn't cry or yell, they bit. And bit hard.

I yanked my tail out of Adrienne's grasp and jumped nimbly onto her thin, gray shoulder. "Take deep breaths. There's no need to panic. Everyone here is a friend. We all want you happy and married to the wonderful Joel. Isn't that what you want, too?"

"I want Zandra here." Adrienne huffed a growl.

"So do I." Desperately so. It had been three weeks since my witch vanished without a trace, taking with her the stones containing most of my ancient magic. Since then, I'd cast every spell imaginable, and I couldn't find her. Our bond was there, so I knew she was alive. But wherever Zandra was, she was hiding, and doing such an excellent job, I'd failed to locate her and help her come to her senses in time for the wedding.

A low growl caught my attention. Joel had his arms out and was shuffling toward Barney Hoffman in a most alarming manner. If I didn't know better, I'd think Joel wanted to take a bite out of one of Barney's beefy arms. And Barney hadn't noticed the danger he was in since he was smiling warmly at Adrienne as she inched closer to the altar.

Barney's familiar, Ember Dreamscape, sprang into action, batting Joel away with a few well-aimed spells and sending the smartly dressed groom back to his position by the flower dressed arch.

We needed to get these ghouls married, so everybody calmed down and no one got munched on.

Joel growled again, but a quick flick of a spell from me drew his attention to Adrienne. The growling stopped, and he smiled, his grasping hands falling to his sides. That was better.

We reached the end of the short aisle, and I handed Adrienne to Joel. "Take the best care of her. I'll be watching to make sure you do."

Joel wasn't much of a talker, but he had an expressive face and was quick to nod at me as he caught hold of Adrienne's hands before giving her a quick kiss on the cheek.

"That's enough! Plenty of time for that later," Cythera scolded. "Kissing happens at the end of this shamb — ceremony."

I left the happy couple and hopped onto a chair. Sage had her seat next to mine. She was curled into a tight ball, looking asleep. But I knew otherwise. Sage hadn't slept soundly for weeks. She'd been a sad, bedraggled mess ever since my horrific, soul-spearing discovery that Zandra had vanished. Because not only had Zandra vanished, but Vorana was gone, too. They'd disappeared at the same time, leaving us behind.

And although I'd had a dreadful shock at learning this miserable truth, Sage had sunk into a deep vat of sludgy depression, often refusing to leave her bed for days.

It had taken all of my persuasive powers to get her out of the house to come to this wedding. Only the promise of a free salmon mousse fountain convinced her it was worth showing her furry face.

I prodded Sage with a paw. "Make an effort and look happy. The ceremony will be over soon."

"This is me making an effort." Sage lifted her head and blearily blinked. "I heard the music. I see the bride and groom. I also haven't broken wind."

"Try to smile. They don't want miserable guests at their wedding."

"I'm allowed to be miserable. My heart is broken. Smooshed and blasted with ice. There's nothing left of it. And if there were, I'd feed it to the ghouls. I don't want it anymore. What use is a heart if it only gets shattered?"

I patted my grumpy friend on the side with a velvet paw. Mine was just as warped out of shape. I was putting on a brave face, but my wonderful witch had gone. It was unthinkable.

Zandra had acted strangely for days before pulling this vanishing act, but I never considered she'd up and leave so suddenly. I'd replayed the events of the days in the lead-up to her disappearance so many times, and I couldn't figure out what had happened. And although I was normally proud of having such a powerful witch by my side, that power was my undoing, because I couldn't find her. Zandra Crypt was stronger than me. And I was weaker for having lost her.

"Dearly gifted magic users and friends, we are gathered here today to join together this ghoul, Adrienne, and this ghoul, Joel, in magical matrimony," Cythera said.

Adrienne and Joel growled in unison. I had to assume it was a happy growl. I wasn't tuned in to the nuanced growls of ghouls.

Cythera glanced at the guests. "I'll keep the ceremony short because I can tell some of you are hungry."

There were a few quiet laughs.

"It'll soon be unlimited salmon mousse fountain time," I whispered to Sage. "That's something to look forward to."

"I'll probably spill mine all over my fur," she grumbled. "Or drown in it. And I don't have Vorana to bathe me afterward. I used to pretend I hated baths, but I didn't. Vorana was so gentle with me, and I always smelled amazing. Maybe that's why she abandoned me. I didn't show her enough appreciation at bath time."

"It's not that." Life hadn't been easy since Zandra and Vorana had vanished. I'd come to rely on both of them for so many things. Zandra was my wonderful companion and sidekick, and Vorana gifted me her cheerful optimism, excellent book recommendations, and had an ability to whip up a feast at a moment's notice.

A rustling in the bushes caught my attention, and I tensed. Was it Zandra? Was she sneaking into the wedding so she wouldn't disturb the ceremony?

I scowled. It was nothing but a basic brown rabbit. The creature saw the crowd and instantly vanished. Sensible choice.

"If there are no objections to the couple being joined together, I'll move on to declaring them magically married," Cythera said.

There was a small amount of shuffling, but everyone was happy Adrienne and Joel were to unite. Adrienne's previous romantic entanglements hadn't gone well, and although she'd gotten Zandra as a result of one of those encounters, her dating history could go in a book of all the things not to do to get your happily ever after.

There were more growls from Adrienne and Joel as vows and rings were exchanged. Adrienne very carefully placed a ring on Joel's finger, since his joints were prone to dislocating and bloating. He did the same to her.

"It gives me the greatest pleasure to present you with the newlywed ghouls, Adrienne and Joel. Joel, you may now kiss your bride," Cythera said. Before she'd even finished her last words, she was stepping away from the altar and checking her watch again.

Cythera had always been on the wrong side of blunt. But lately, she'd been downright unpleasant to be around and often delighted in whacking me with her giant wings for no good reason. I had several bruises to show for it.

The ghouls kissed, and there was a quiet round of applause from the guests.

"Can I go back to bed now?" Sage asked.

"Mingling and salmon mousse first. You only have to stay for half an hour. Besides, Adrienne and Joel have a special treat arranged as part of their honeymoon," I said. "Cannibal Bill has been collecting all the best bits of offal and will be placing them around the woods for them to hunt. They'll have such a fun night."

"That sounds gory and disgusting," Sage said. "Count me out."

"Fortunately for you, none of us are invited on the honeymoon. And I wouldn't expect you to go offal hunting, not when there's a bottomless fountain of salmon mousse with your name on it. No chewing required."

Sage grumbled some more but dragged her disheveled self off of the cushion and flopped onto the ground.

There was more rustling in the bushes. The rabbit had returned. This time, it had a companion. I shooed them away, but they ignored me, instead hopping toward the bride and groom. Did they have a death wish?

Joel spotted them first. His eyes flashed, and his teeth snapped.

I leapt in front of the rabbits. "No! These aren't your wedding feast. We have an outdoor table set up a short walk away with everything you need. The slaughterhouse provided so many treats. So did Cannibal Bill. And Tia made you an offal cake with royal icing. There are three tiers. All for you."

Joel growled again, and this time, Adrienne joined him, her gaze glazing over when she spotted the bunnies.

I flared magic around me in a warning. "Look away from the rabbits. Emotions are running high, but you must control yourselves."

They didn't hear me, and the growling grew worse, the ghouls' fingers flexing as they drooled and swiped their feet through the dirt as if building up the energy to burst into a run.

My magic flared brighter. "This is your final warning! I don't want my wedding gift to you to be a night in the cells for ghoulish bad behavior."

"Get your ghouls under control!" Cythera yelled, her wings unfurled and her hands in fists. "I told you this was a dumb idea."

Joel's head whipped around at the sound of Cythera's angry tone. He coiled like a spring and leapt at her.

Chapter 2

Wedding jinx

The tension snapped like a taut wire as Joel lunged at Cythera, his growl a guttural rumble that sent shivers down my spine. I flew into action, my fur bristling with the surge of magic coursing through me.

"Sage, we've got to stop them!" My voice carried over the ghouls' snarls and groans. "Everyone else, get out of here. And whatever you do, don't get bitten."

The few wedding guests who lingered didn't need telling twice. Everyone knew what happened if you got a ghoul's teeth attached to you.

Sage, her fur standing on end like a field of quills, nodded grimly as she settled in beside me, ready to do battle.

I focused on my magic, feeling the familiar warmth build in my chest before I released it in a burst of energy aimed at Adrienne. The force of the spell knocked her back, but she was on her feet in an instant, eyes blazing with a feral hunger. She lunged at me, her movements unnaturally fast for someone who looked so fragile.

With a quick, agile twist, I dodged her attack and countered with a wave of magic that sent her sprawling.

Beside me, Sage was locked in a battle with Joel. Her spells were powerful, but Joel seemed almost invulnerable, shrugging off her attacks with a terrifying ease. He snapped at her, jaws closing inches from her tail as she darted out of reach, her harness whacking him hard in the thigh and making him roar with unhappiness.

"Juno, a little help here!" Desperation crept into Sage's voice as she knocked over chairs while fleeing Joel's dogged pursuit. "This ghoul's been working out. I can't outrun him."

I couldn't afford to let Adrienne get up again. With a swift incantation, I bound her in glowing chains of magic, the tendrils wrapping around her limbs and holding her in place, then turned my attention to Joel.

Sage was throwing everything she had at him, her magic crackling through the air like tiny bolts of lightning. I joined her, our combined power slamming into Joel and sending him reeling.

For a moment, it seemed like we had the upper paw, but then Joel let out a bone-chilling roar and charged at us, eyes wild with rage.

"You've made him angry by chaining his bride." Sage hissed at Joel.

We synchronized our attacks, our spells weaving into a net of energy that ensnared Joel. He thrashed against it, snarling and snapping, but the more he struggled, the tighter the net became.

I looked around for any help from Cythera. She was leaning against a tree, inspecting her fingernails, the rabbits sitting by her feet, watching the fight. What was wrong with this staunch, rule abiding angel? She was always the first to stop any disputes.

Adrienne, sensing Joel's predicament, let out a furious groan and strained against her bonds. The chains wavered, and I knew I couldn't hold both of them for long. I split my focus, reinforcing Adrienne's bonds even as I kept the net around Joel intact.

Joel's snarls grew louder, more desperate, as he realized he was trapped. His eyes met mine, and for a moment, I saw a flicker of something human in them—a plea, perhaps, or a memory of who he used to be. But it was gone in an instant, replaced by the mindless rage of a ghoul who only wanted to destroy.

With a final surge of magic, Sage and I tightened the net, binding Joel and Adrienne into a cocoon of shimmering energy. They thrashed and snarled, but they were securely trapped.

Panting, I looked at Sage and nodded. But the victory was bittersweet. Adrienne and Joel were more than just ghouls—they were part of our community, our family, and now they were lost to us. Their minds consumed by a monstrous hunger that turned them against the people who cared for them.

"We only just stopped them. And with no help from the angels." Sage glared at Cythera. "What is she playing at?"

"That's a question for another time. Why did the ghouls react like this?" I knocked Adrienne back down as she struggled to get to her feet.

"Maybe they considered the rabbits a honeymoon treat," Sage said. "Or maybe they wanted to hunt and destroy anything they liked the look of. A wedding gift to each other."

A glance in Cythera's direction, and I could see she was finally paying attention. Her wings were flared, her blue eyes sparking with anger, and her hands in fists.

"I knew this was a mistake." Cythera marched over to join us. "Ghouls cannot be controlled."

"They got excited by the rabbits," I said. "And with all the wedding nerves flying around and guest excitement, it's no surprise a couple of long-eared fluffballs tipped things over the edge."

Cythera glared down at the trapped ghouls. "I should never have agreed to be involved in this embarrassing mess. I could have predicted this would happen."

"Let's put this down to wedding overexcitement and move on," I said.

"Move on, how exactly?" Cythera jabbed a finger at Joel. "These creatures are out of control. You let them loose to party and we'll have a bloodbath on our hands."

"They're not creatures! They're valuable members of our community."

"Valuable to whom?" Cythera said. "Ghouls are classed as dangerous creatures that must be destroyed."

I hissed softly, edging round to form a block between Cythera and our captives. "You're not destroying Zandra's mother and her new stepfather."

"Zandra won't know. She's not here anymore. And even if she was, she wouldn't care. A ghoul for a mother is humiliating," Cythera said. "Hand them over. We'll deal with them back at Angel Force."

I hissed again. "You're not destroying them. They're a part of my family and therefore under my protection."

"Our protection." Sage stood beside me, her hackles raised.

"Then I'll lock you up with them. You won't consider the bond you have with these monsters familial once they bite you." Cythera sneered at me, exposing perfect white shiny teeth. Somehow, they looked unnatural.

"Keep your hands off my ghouls," I said. "They've just gotten married. You can't destroy their happiness."

Cythera swept a wing over my head. "They're unsafe to remain free. This is for their own good."

I remained in place. "I'm surprised you even care. I've barely seen you at Angel Force these past few weeks."

"That's none of your concern," Cythera said. "Give me those ghouls."

"They stay with me and Sage. We'll look after them and make sure they're properly secured and can't harm anybody."

"Not acceptable."

Someone clearing their throat close by caught my attention. Roland Moldsworth and his familiar, Nimbus, stood to one side, watching the scene with wide eyes.

"Um... Is this a bad time?" Roland asked.

"Always. What is it?" Cythera snapped.

"I'm sorry to intrude on this, err... unfortunate situation." Roland's nervous gaze flicked to the ghouls, and he gulped. "But I needed to speak to you urgently about the festival."

"Now? What about it?" Cythera asked. "Every time you come to the office, it's all mushroom this, fungi that, toadstool whatever. Get the festival over with and leave me alone."

"Of course. I'm sorry to be such a pest. And you've been so generous with lending us your angels for the event." Roland's voice quivered.

Cythera flicked a glance at him, and her anger faded. "My team is looking forward to it. Those who aren't there in an official capacity will be able to let their hair down."

"There seems to be a lot of that happening recently. I've never seen your angels party so much." I pressed a paw on Adrienne's leg as she began to growl again.

"Keep out of this, fluffy," Cythera said. "What my angels do in their private time is none of your business. You always have to poke your wet nose into matters that don't concern you."

"I expect you're glad I did this time. Otherwise, the wedding party would be turning into ghouls. You didn't lift a finger to help when Adrienne and Joel became feisty."

"As you said, they're your family. Your problem. I'll deal with the cleanup. Same as always."

"No cleanup," I said.

"I... I am sorry to butt in again," Roland said, "but I'm anxious the festival is a success. Given how unstable everything seems in Crimson Cove..." His gaze went back to the ghouls, and he shivered.

"Unstable? There's nothing unstable about this boring little town," Cythera said. "And if you're worried about these ghouls being a problem, don't be. They'll be destroyed by the end of the day."

"To destroy them, you'll have to get through me." My words came out as a whispered threat. I didn't want to obliterate Cythera, but if she kept on like this, she'd leave me no choice.

Cythera smirked. "That's a challenge I accept."

"Enough!" Sage shot out a spell that smacked Cythera squarely on the side of her head. "You've always been a stick up the butt jerk, but never spiteful. These ghouls don't deserve to be put down. Leave them in a cell for a couple of nights and let them cool off. They'll soon realize their mistake. If you destroy them, you'll be breaking rules and hearts, and there's too much of that going on lately."

"Who are you to tell me what to do?" Cythera rubbed the side of her head. "I thought you were about to shuffle off into the pet cemetery, anyway.

You've done nothing but mope around since Vorana abandoned you."

"She hasn't abandoned me. And when she comes back, I want the town to be just as she left it." Sage hissed fiercely, another spell shimmering on one paw, ready to let fly if Cythera kept fighting us.

"Minus all the misbehaving and weirdness," I muttered, secretly pleased my friend was showing some gumption. She'd been acting like she'd given up and was waiting to die ever since Vorana had vanished with Zandra.

"Yes, of course. Minus all the weirdness," Sage snapped back. "Besides, Vorana likes Adrienne. She helped plan this wedding. She'd be devastated if this was the end result."

"If you don't mind me putting in my two cents, the ghouls seem calmer," Roland said. "Perhaps Juno and Sage are right. They got overexcited because this was such an exhilarating event. I wouldn't be able to stand still on my wedding day. I'd be so full of nervous excitement."

"Are you planning on getting married soon?" Cythera asked.

"No! I'm content with it being me and Nimbus. It's been the two of us for such a long time that it would take an extraordinary person to change things. Isn't that right, Nimbus? We're happy together, aren't we?"

Nimbus growled and hissed, making it clear what she thought about Roland finding a romantic partner and potentially displacing his affections.

Cythera sighed. "I could do without the extra paperwork. Destroying a ghoul requires reams of the stuff to be filled in. And I want to attend your festival. I heard there'll be fungi wine and truffles."

"Oh! Yes! All the wine and velvety truffles you can manage. And all for free for our wonderful Angel Force." Roland pressed his hands together. "And the more angels, the better. Just in case... well, you know." He gestured at the ghouls.

"Does that mean you won't be destroying the happy couple, after all?" I asked Cythera.

She glared at the ghouls for a long, silent minute. "I'm taking them in. They can stay in the cells until I figure out what to do with them. I'm not having my plans messed up because these two can't keep control of themselves."

Given the weird mood Cythera had been in recently, I didn't trust her. "I'll need to see them every day. And I'll expect updates. As their closest family, I must know what you have planned for them."

"Cythera will do the right thing by these two... charming creatures," Roland said. "She's been so supportive of the fungi festival. It'll be the biggest, boldest event ever seen in Crimson Cove."

"That's an impressive statement, given the focus is on mushrooms," I said coolly, my nerves frayed and my patience thin after everything that had just happened.

"But mushrooms are magical," Roland said. "And I've uncovered rare finds in Crimson Cove. I'm thrilled I've made this my new home. Before you know it, the town will become the fungi capital of the world. Imagine that."

"I'm trying." I whacked another sedation spell on Adrienne because she was getting feisty again. "Cythera, perhaps you could gently escort Adrienne and Joel to a safe cell and ensure they're well looked after?"

She flipped me a salute. "Always happy to take orders from you."

I wrinkled my booping snooter. "Sarcasm is an ill-fitting garment on your feathered form. I'll come with you to make sure they're settled. And they'll need regular feeding, or they'll lose control."

"There's the wedding food," Sage said. "We could take it to the cells to make sure Adrienne and Joel don't get hungry."

"That's an excellent idea," I said. "We'll take their wedding cake. That'll keep them busy for a while."

"Will I see you at the festival?" Roland asked me, seeming only able to focus on his upcoming mushroom event.

"I'm not in the mood to party," I said. "I may drop by, but for a few moments."

"Oh! Of course. That was thoughtless of me. I understand you may not be in the happiest of moods. I was sorry to hear that your witch vanished." Roland rested a hand on Nimbus. "Nimbus was telling me all about it. Such a sad business. Do you know when she'll return?"

"Very soon," I said. "Any day now."

"That'll be something to rejoice," Roland said. "I don't know what I'd do if Nimbus left me. Curl up in a ball and cry myself to sleep every night."

"Zandra hasn't left me. She had urgent business to attend to out of town." The quiver in my voice gave me away.

Cythera barked a hard laugh. "You keep telling yourself that, fluff 'n' stuff. But you'll soon have to admit that your bond with Zandra wasn't enough to keep her by your side. She must have gotten a better offer."

I turned my back on her and carefully inspected Adrienne. Her beautiful wedding dress was smeared with dirt, and her makeup streaked down her face, forming two black lines on her cheeks. "You must get control of yourself. You don't want to be destroyed just after you've gotten married. You have your whole future with Joel to look forward to. Focus on that. And stop snapping your teeth at me."

Adrienne grumbled what may have been an apology or possibly a cuss word.

"Well, I must be off," Roland said. "Everything is starting tonight, and I want to make sure I haven't missed any important details. We could have sold double the number of tickets for the talks and demonstrations. It'll be spectacular. I hope you can all make it."

"We'll see," I murmured.

Roland spoke to Cythera for a few moments about Angel Force security at the event and then bustled off with Nimbus wrapped around his shoulders.

After more sharp words with Cythera and the careful application of control magic, Adrienne and Joel were finally on their feet, their hands bound and masks placed over their noses and mouths so they couldn't bite anyone. It was an unfortunate end to what should have been a magical day.

I walked behind Cythera as she herded the ghouls through the forest back to town.

"We'll watch over them." Sage walked beside me. "Make sure the angels do nothing dumb."

"I'm worried. Angel Force has been doing too many foolish things recently. And it'll break Zandra's heart when she comes back and finds her mother destroyed because she got overexcited on her wedding day."

Sage glanced at me. "Any idea when she'll come back?"

"Soon. I guarantee it." I wished that were true. Where was my wonderful witch when I needed her the most, and what had gone so badly wrong that she'd abandoned me?

Chapter 3

Mushroom surprise

"Help me move this ottoman." I bumped my head against the dented wooden box with a red velvet topped lid.

Sammy poked his head out of the closet then hopped out and joined me. "We've searched this house a dozen times. If your magical stones were still here, we'd have found them by now. You always tell me you can sense their power. If you can't sense it now, that means they're gone."

"We haven't looked under here. I'm not giving up. Help me."

Sammy, my sweet furry companion, used his considerable bulk to shove the ottoman to one side.

I sighed. All that was under there were a few dust bunnies and an old candy wrapper. "I'll look inside. The stones could have been tucked under something I missed the first time."

Sammy twitched his whiskers. "We tipped everything out of this ottoman, and we didn't find your stones. They're gone. Zandra took them with her."

"Why would she do such a thing?" I was already inside the ottoman, scrabbling through piles of scratchy woolen blankets. "She has no idea what is inside those stones. They mean nothing to her."

Sammy rested his chin on the edge of the ottoman. "Even those of us who don't have great power sense something special about your stones."

I glanced up at him. "You have great power."

"It's better than it used to be. But that's not what I meant. Your magic is something else. Something none of us can hold a candle to. Whenever I'm around you, it always gives me the shivers."

"In a good way?"

"In a great way. That's why I know those stones aren't here. They're nowhere near this house. Most likely, not even in Crimson Cove."

"I'm not giving up until I find them. I've almost made my decision about what to do with them." I reached the bottom of the ottoman, but there was no sign of the stones.

"Look on the bright side. The stones are gone, so your decision has been made for you. There's no dilemma to ponder."

I hated that idea. "What if I want to access all of my magic again? I could have decided to absorb it and return to my former life. You'd have come with me, of course."

Sammy tilted his head. "Would I? I'm happy here. I'm happy with the way my life is going. I don't want things to change."

"Things never stay the same, even when we want them to." I clambered out of the ottoman. "What have we missed? Some nook or cranny where my stones have been hidden."

"We need a break." Sammy followed me out of Vorana's bedroom. "The mushroom festival will have started by now. We should go take a look. It could be fun. You remember what it was like to have fun, don't you?"

"Why are you so interested in mushrooms?" I checked in Vorana's private bathroom, but it was just as I'd left it. No secret stash of stones had been deposited in the sink.

"I'm not. But the festival sounds incredible. I heard there'll be free food and drink samples. You could fill your belly and not worry about foraging for dinner tonight. Take a night off and relax."

I paused, considering his words. "I don't want to relax. I want Zandra and my stones back in the basement."

Sammy stood in front of me, blocking my path to the stairs. "I know. But there's nothing you can do about either of those things. Wherever Zandra is, she doesn't want you to find her. And that hurts, but you need to give her time."

"Time to forget about me? Time to forget she has a happy life here with friends and family surrounding her?" I shook my head. "Zandra must be back by my side. Our bond is distorted, and that distortion is only growing worse. I have to get her back so I can fix things."

"It would do Sage good to get out of the house," Sammy said. "I'm worried about her. She's given up the will to live. Every time I come around, she's asleep or staring out of the window, looking sad."

"She's devastated Vorana has gone. And that makes no sense either." I sidled around Sammy but paused before I descended the stairs. "Perhaps Zandra and Vorana were taken. They were forced to leave Crimson Cove against their will."

"Who would want to take them?" Sammy followed me down the stairs.

"Whoever it was, they must be immensely powerful and ridiculously stupid. When I get my paws on them, there'll be nothing left."

"Were there signs of a struggle?"

"No."

"And didn't you say Zandra packed all her clothes? Would her mysterious abductor have done that?"

"Stop complicating things."

"I'm not. But you can't make up worst-case scenarios. Especially not around Sage. She's too fragile. Until we figure out exactly what went on, let's take a time out."

"I don't want a time out."

Sammy gently tugged my tail. "Do it for Sage. We need to get her to see there's still joy in the world." He stopped by the kitchen. Sage was pretending to sleep on the prickly mat by the back door. "If we're not busy living, then we're standing in place and waiting to die. That's wrong. And it's unfair on all of us. I know you have problems and you're sad, but an hour off will give your mind a rest from ruminating on those problems. It could even give you clarity."

I didn't like to admit it, but Sammy had a valid argument.

"I don't want or need clarity," Sage grumbled. "Leave me out of whatever dumb thing you're planning."

"It's decided. And you're coming with us even if I have to drag you by the scruff." Sammy stomped over to the prickly mat. He nudged Sage hard with his head. "Get up and stop feeling sorry for yourself. You too, Juno. We've all got complications in our lives, but that doesn't mean we can't still enjoy things. Up! Up now."

I let out an exhausted sigh. Was I wasting my time looking around the house again for the stones? I had looked everywhere and used dozens of spells to find them, and they were as gone as my wonderful witch.

Had Zandra really taken them? I didn't want to believe it, but it seemed the most logical explanation. I still couldn't understand why, though. Did she realize there was something special about them and wanted the magic for herself? I hoped she didn't try to access it. She was an immensely powerful witch, but all that intensely compressed magic would destroy her if she opened it all at once without realizing what was inside the stones.

"She's up!" Sammy said as Sage rolled to her paws. "Get in your harness. Fresh air and free food are exactly what we all need."

"When did you become so cheerfully, and may I say irritatingly, optimistic?" Sage grudgingly got herself into her harness. "We always have to cajole you to do anything even mildly brave."

"I turned over a new leaf," Sammy said. "You should too. No more moping."

"I'll mope if I like."

"Not tonight. Tonight, we're going fungi foraging."

A few minutes later, we were heading toward the raucous sounding festival. I was surprised by how popular such an event was. There were hundreds of unfamiliar faces heading in the same direction as us, toward the bright marquees and music.

"You see! I told you the event would be good." Sammy's eyes were bright with excitement as he scanned the marquees. Most were selling food and drink, but some had jars of ointments and lotions. A few sold mushroom-themed trinkets. There were also clothes stands and crystals.

"Who's the guy with the cloak that's covered in mushrooms?" Sage was looking around, her nose wrinkled. "He looks like a dork."

"Excuse me for overhearing, but you must know our esteemed mushroom mage," said a tall, thin-lipped man of around fifty who stood beside us. He wore a cloak similar to the mushroom dork, but it was black with embroidered mushrooms around the hem.

"We're new to the world of fungi," I said. "Who is he?"

"The master of ceremonies. Our Grand Mushroom Mage, Kinoko Sporeleigh." There was a sneering tone in the stranger's voice.

"I see you're into your mushrooms, too," I said.

He bowed low, sweeping one arm out. "They are my life. Gilly Piper, at your service. I lecture on all things fungi. I'm a renowned expert."

"Fancy that," Sage said. "Tell me one interesting thing about mushrooms."

Gilly's eyes narrowed a fraction, as if he sensed the sarcasm. "There are too many fascinating facts to know where to begin. But since you're at this festival, you must have open minds to the spectacular possibilities of how fungi will change your world."

"We came for the free food," Sage said.

"And it will be excellent food. Just don't get carried away eating too much of the magically infused fungi, or you could end up floating away."

"That sounds like an excellent idea," Sage grumbled. "Show me to the floaty mushroom stand so I can stuff myself and float home."

"I told you, I don't want you here!" A younger man strode past wearing an elaborately decorated mushroom shaped hat with a pointed tip. He was accompanied by a skinny older man with long dark hair and a red tattoo running down one side of his face. Other than the tattoo, they were so similar in feature that I had to assume they were related.

"I'm not here to cause trouble. I just want to see my famous son in action." The older man's voice was a hoarse croak, suggesting he was recovering from an illness.

"Go home. This is no place for you. I have a packed schedule, and I can't afford to be disturbed."

"I'll only stay to watch your talk. I'll cause no problems."

"Who's the man wearing the mushroom hat?" I asked as the arguing men scurried away.

"Don't waste your time with him. He's nothing special." Gilly scowled at the men, suggesting he was appalled to find them at the festival.

"The younger guy said he was giving a talk. He must be special enough to be booked to make a presentation."

Gilly grimaced. "Azureus Stool. Alleged fungi expert and general joke. He never took a course in his life and is only self-taught. A self-taught buffoon, more like. I don't know how Azureus does it, but he's fooled everyone into thinking he's the foremost expert on anything fungi-related. I spent six years studying for my degree in Fungiology, yet some upstart who's read a few pop culture books on fungi and has a winning smile gets the best gigs. It's a disgrace."

"Jealous much?" Sage asked.

"It's not jealousy. It's frustration," Gilly said. "Azureus doesn't deserve to be here. And he definitely doesn't deserve to give the keynote speech. He'll make a mockery of mushrooms."

Roland Moldsworth and Nimbus dashed past, a nervy elf scurrying beside them. Roland slowed when he saw us and gave a quick wave. "I'm so happy you came. I can't stop. A million and one things to do and no time to do them. Enjoy!"

"Likewise, I'm also busy." Gilly swept another bow before turning away. "Relish the fungi."

"Who knew the world of mushrooms was so intense?" Sammy said. "Professional rivalries and family squabbles. This should be an exciting event."

"I'm not staying long enough to immerse myself in any drama," I said. "An hour at the most."

"You never know, you may enjoy yourself," Sammy said. "Let's look at the stalls. We'll get some samples and take it from there."

I trudged behind Sammy with Sage beside me. Despite the infectious air of joy and excitement, I didn't feel a single tingle of happiness. Everything felt pointless now Zandra had gone. I missed her snide comments and her comfortable shoulder to sit on so I could see everything, without risking getting my glorious tail trodden on by over-enthusiastic fungi fiends.

"They're giving out free food during this talk!" Sammy gestured to a marquee people were trickling into.

"The Wonderful World of Fungi: Its mysteries revealed," I read off the sign outside. "As long as it's warm and there's food, let's take a look."

An hour later, I had to admit, the fungi talk had been fascinating. I learned about their ability to heal each other, the powerful medicinal properties of certain types of fungi, and fungi that attacked when threatened. It was incredible what went on beneath our paws. There had also been generous platters of food, and although Sammy had tucked in, I had no appetite for nibbles.

Sammy nudged me. "Will you admit you had a good time?"

"It was an interesting talk," I said.

"But you're still sad?"

"And I'll remain sad until Zandra is back," I said. "You don't have a bond with anyone, but you know what it's like. That special, unique connection with one person that runs so deep, you never want it to end. I'm sick with worry about what's happened to her."

"Are you sure Zandra's family hasn't seen her?" Sammy polished off the last of the treats on the platter of food left on the seat beside him.

"They don't know where she is. And I didn't want to alarm them by saying she's gone missing."

"You should alarm them! Get a gang of Crypt witches on your side, hunting for Zandra. They'd know if she's hiding somewhere. They can do anything."

I had been thinking about getting Zandra's family involved in the search. They were a quirky bunch of witches, and as powerful as many a demigoddess. But what if Zandra had abandoned me and made them promise not to say anything? I didn't know any of the Crypt witches well enough to know if they were telling me the truth.

"I'm worried about you," Sammy said softly. "I miss the old Juno."

"She'll be back once my missing witch is home," I said. "I'm not giving up looking for Zandra. Even if I find her and she confirms my worst fears that she wants nothing to do with me, then so be it. But I must know the truth."

"Can we go to bed yet?" Sage asked, breaking through our tense conversation.

"Let's have one more look around the stalls," Sammy said. "There might be more free food."

"Another ten minutes," I whispered to Sage. "Then we're going home."

She grumbled as she trudged behind us, barely pausing to look at the display of crystal mushrooms and the oil diffusers with their different, earthy mushroom scents.

By the time we reached the end of the long row, the crowd was slowly thinning as people made their way home, their arms full of goodies and their bellies full of food. The first night of the festival had been a roaring success.

"Before we go home, we must visit Adrienne and Joel at Angel Force," I said as I looked for the quickest way out, "to make sure Cythera has done nothing stupid."

"I wouldn't put anything past that surly grump," Sage said. "Fine. A quick stop but then home to bed."

I looked around for Sammy to let him know where we were going, but he was deep in conversation with a stallholder, looking at a range of mushroom shaped soaps.

A cry of alarm caught my attention, and I nudged Sage into action to find out what was going on. The noise took me behind one of the smaller marquees.

"You always follow trouble." Sage lurked behind me, huffing her displeasure. "Let someone else deal with this."

"Whoever cried out could need help."

"Then let someone else help!"

"There's no one else. There'll all looking at the weird mushroom stuff."

Sage grumbled about me sticking my nose in where it wasn't wanted. She sounded just like Cythera.

I arrived at the back of the marquee to discover Roland and Nimbus standing over a body.

Chapter 4

Deadly surprise

"What's going on?" I dashed toward Roland, Sage close behind me.

Nimbus, her enormous tongue lashing out at me like a whip, stood guard, preventing me from reaching Roland or the man on the ground.

I reared back, avoiding being covered in Nimbus's saliva. "Roland! Who is that? Is he hurt?"

Roland's panicked gaze met mine. He swayed from side to side and fainted.

Nimbus jumped off Roland's shoulder just before he hit the ground. She rolled several times, her white fur fluffed out in a threat display.

I took another step toward Roland, but Nimbus bared her teeth. "Stay back."

"Calm yourself. We're not here to hurt Roland, but we need to know if that person on the ground next to him needs help."

"Dead, he is," Nimbus said. "Won't be able to save. No help needed."

"I'll get Cythera," Sage muttered before dashing away.

I lifted a paw to get closer, but a warning growl from Nimbus made me freeze. "I understand you feel the need to protect Roland, but you know me. I don't want to harm him."

"Trust no one, we do. Everyone lies and betrays."

"I don't. And I'm offended you think that about me." Despite attempting several ways to get around Nimbus to see to the man lying face down in the dirt, she refused to relent, hissing and snarling every time I made a move.

"What's going on?" Cythera strode over with Bertoli, Sage behind them. "Your smelly, fluffy friend said someone's been hurt."

"It's more than that," I said, "but Nimbus is refusing to let me see the body."

"Body! Someone's dead? Get out of my way. Let me see what trouble you've caused this time." Cythera yelped and staggered back as Nimbus launched herself at the giant angel, her teeth attaching to one wing and shaking it.

"I should have warned you about Nimbus's protective streak." I dodged out of the way as Cythera and Nimbus battled. "She thinks we want to hurt Roland. Nothing I could say settled her."

"What's wrong with Roland?" Bertoli made no move to assist Cythera as he took in the scene as calmly as if he was watching paint dry.

"He fainted. I think he just discovered the body. I heard him yell and came to investigate."

"Are you sure the man in the dirt is dead?" Bertoli asked.

"That's what I'm trying to find out, but as you can see, Nimbus is proving to be a problem."

Cythera succeeded in dislodging Nimbus from her wing. She held her at arm's length as Nimbus thrashed and snarled. "I'll have you destroyed if you keep misbehaving."

"No! She's worried about Roland. That's why she's behaving so strangely. Nimbus, go sit with Roland and make sure he's safe. I promise we won't touch him," I said.

Nimbus growled some more, snapping her teeth dangerously close to Cythera's nose.

"I suggest you let her go," I said to Cythera. "She'll only get angrier if you keep her away from Roland."

"She's a menace! You work for animal control. Can't you do something? You must carry sedation darts."

"Sadly, my lack of pockets or utility belt prevents that solution. Let her go back to Roland and she'll be fine," I said. "You'll behave, won't you, Nimbus?"

All I got was a growling snarl in response.

After a few more seconds of struggle, Cythera dropped Nimbus. She landed nimbly and scuttled to Roland, lying full length on his belly, her face resting close to his as she sniffled his chin.

"This guy is definitely dead," Bertoli said. He'd been peering at the body. He'd even turned the man over before inspecting the scene for signs of foul play. "It looks like he's been strangled. See these red marks around his neck?"

Cythera strolled over and made a cursory inspection of the body. "I don't know him. He's not local."

I inched closer. "I do. Not personally, but I saw him give a talk this evening about fungi. His name is Azureus Stool. I'm assuming as in toadstool, not footstool. He's one of the experts Roland brought in for the festival."

"He's not an expert anymore," Bertoli said. "He'll soon be fertilizing the mushrooms, not collecting them."

Cythera chuckled. "Probably the best thing for him if he's obsessed with toadstools. What a loser."

The angels laughed. They were actually laughing over a dead body.

"Aren't you concerned a man has been murdered?" I asked.

"It was probably an overexcited festival-goer. Nobody who lives here," Cythera said. "And they'll be long gone by now."

"Or maybe not." I prodded Azureus's body. It was warm. "He's not been dead for long. If we can rouse Roland, he may have seen something. He may even know who the killer is, and you can catch them before they leave Crimson Cove."

"Or Roland is the killer," Bertoli said. "He was caught red-handed, and he's faking his faint while he gets his story together."

Nimbus hissed. "Untruths, you speak. Lies come from the mouth. Seal it shut, I shall."

Bertoli shrugged. "I'm going to see if there are any of those miniature sweet mushroom pies left. I had three earlier, and they were delicious."

"Get me one," Cythera said. "And some of those truffles from the stall with the pink flag."

I stared at them in disbelief, although I shouldn't be surprised by their nonchalant attitude toward a murder. Angel Force had barely been open these past few weeks. The angels were either on vacation or simply not turning up for work. I'd questioned Cythera about it several times, but she'd shooed me out of the office with plenty of rude gestures and insults.

"Actually, I'll come with you," Cythera said. "Juno, you love to poke around in business that doesn't concern you, so you can handle this, can't you?"

"It seems I have no choice." My attention was already on the body, since it was clear I'd get little help from Angel Force to solve this crime. "Send me some backup, though. We'll need to search for the murder weapon."

Cythera stuck her fingers in her mouth and whistled. A few seconds later, two angels descended from the sky. She gave them their instructions and then walked off with Bertoli.

I shook my head, not hiding my disappointment at such indifferent behavior. Just like so many other things in this town, Angel Force was broken. I instructed the newly arrived angels to look around for an obvious murder weapon. Whatever had been used to strangle Azureus would be long and thin. Perhaps a belt or a piece of rope.

They wandered off, making a half-hearted effort to look around the area behind the marquee.

Roland groaned, and his eyes flickered open. "What happened?"

I stayed where I was, aware Nimbus would strike if I made any move she considered inappropriate. "If I'm interpreting the scene correctly, you found Azureus's body, and then you fainted."

Roland jerked upright, one hand going around Nimbus so she didn't fall off him. "Azureus! How is he?"

"Very much dead," I said.

Roland blinked rapidly, his breathing growing so shallow, I feared he might faint again.

"Take some deep breaths. You've had a shock. But I need to know what happened."

Roland settled Nimbus on his shoulders. His gaze darted to Azureus's body, and he looked away. "This is terrible. I thought I'd had a nightmare. This can't be happening."

"It is. What can you tell me?" I asked.

Roland did more deep breathing. "I was winding up the festival. I had a few jobs to tick off my list, which included going around the stalls and marquees, making sure everything was tidy, and seeing if the stallholders needed anything for tomorrow. I was checking back here to make sure nothing had been left unattended that could get damaged. That's when I almost tripped over the... the body."

"You were together when this happened?" I addressed the question to Roland and Nimbus.

Roland nodded. "We're never apart. We've been working hard all day. I was exhausted and looking forward to a good night's rest. Now, I don't think I'll get a wink of sleep. I'll keep seeing this horrible scene."

"Better Azureus was found now than his body left here overnight," I said. "And from what I've observed, this has only just happened. What did you see when you found him?"

Roland shuddered. "Nothing! I'd just gotten here when you arrived with Sage. The next thing, I'm waking up on the ground. I'm so embarrassed to have fainted. Some use I am."

"It's not uncommon," I said. "Most people never get to see a dead body. They should be grateful for that."

"It's not something I ever want to see again." Roland found courage and finally looked at Azureus. Tears filled his eyes.

"Did you see anyone running away as you got here?" I asked.

"Running away? Why would they do that?"

"Because Azureus was murdered," I said. "It looks likely he was strangled. There are marks around his neck."

"Oh, dear. I need to lie down." Roland sank into the dirt, making Nimbus scuttle off his shoulders and settle on his chest. "Who would want Azureus dead? He was so popular."

"That's for me to find out," I said. "And Cythera has put me in charge of the investigation since she's more interested in buying truffles than solving crimes."

"There are excellent truffle sellers here," Roland murmured. "What a mess. Have I already said that? But it is. My first fully fledged mushroom festival and someone dies. Worse, they're murdered! And I find the body."

"Azureus was something special in your community, wasn't he?" I asked. "I heard his talk this evening, and I was impressed. He seemed to know everything about fungi."

"Oh, yes. He was the best in the business. So clever and knowledgeable. But more than that, he had a wonderful way of telling a story. He could make the driest facts sound fascinating. That's why I asked him to come to the festival. I wanted everyone to become as enthralled with fungi as I am."

"His talk opened my eyes," I said. "I won't look at the humble mushroom quite the same way ever again."

"Then at least I achieved my goal with one person," Roland said. "Well, cat. Are you really sure his death wasn't an accident? Perhaps he got tangled in a marquee rope and injured himself."

"If that happened, the rope would still be around Azureus's neck." I looked over at the angels to see if they'd made progress with finding the murder weapon. They'd stopped searching and were joking with each other. "As you can see, there's no sign of any rope or belt that could have done this to Azureus. Can you think of anyone who had a grudge against him?"

Roland sat up again, and Nimbus returned to sitting on his shoulders. "When you're at the top of your game, you can put noses out of joint. Professional jealousy is real in our community."

"I never thought about fungi making people passionate," I said. "There were other experts who didn't like Azureus?"

"Yes, there was bad blood," Roland said after a few seconds of hesitation. "People get obsessed about fungi."

"Is there anyone at this festival who didn't like Azureus?"

Roland considered the question as he gently petted Nimbus. "Well, there's Gilly Piper. Have you met him?"

"Briefly. When we first got to the festival, he overheard our conversation and pointed out a few of the key figures."

"They've argued on and off for years," Roland said. "The last argument was over a specific fungus classification. Azureus believed the new fungus found should be under one classification, and Gilly believed it should be another. They even wrote papers attempting to disprove the other's theory. It was an intense debate. Voices were raised on several occasions."

I turned to share an amused look with Zandra, but then remembered she wasn't there. "Would that be something Gilly would kill Azureus over?"

Roland brushed dried mud off his elbow. "I couldn't say. Perhaps. And Gilly covets Azureus's position. Maybe something inside him snapped. Or Azureus goaded Gilly, and he reacted in this terrible way."

"Have you seen them arguing at this festival?"

"No, but I've been busy. I haven't stood still for more than a few seconds. They could have come to blows, and I missed the whole thing."

"Nimbus, did you see anything?" I asked.

"I see what Roland sees. Nothing more. Always together, we are."

That was an unhelpful reply. "You should get home," I said to Roland. "You've had a shock, so take it easy for the rest of the night."

"I do feel lightheaded," Roland said. "But I must be well for tomorrow. We have another sold-out day ahead of us."

"I'm not sure the angels will allow the festival to continue, given someone was murdered," I said. "We'll have to do a full investigation. Currently, we're sitting in the middle of a crime scene."

"Oh! I hadn't thought about that." Roland lifted a shaky hand to his mouth. "I hope they let it go ahead. Everyone's had such a wonderful time."

"Apart from Azureus," I said.

Nimbus hissed at me. "Festival, we will have. Keep nose out, you will. If not, be bitten off."

"It's okay, Nimbus. I'll find Cythera and see what she thinks," Roland said. "You don't mind, do you, Juno? Azureus would want this event to continue. He loved fungi as much as I do, and he wouldn't want everyone's fun to stop because of this tragedy."

"If Cythera says it's fine, I won't stop you," I said.

Roland got to his feet. He wobbled for a few seconds but stayed upright. He dabbed away a tear that trickled down his cheek. "I'm sorry about Azureus. I deeply admired his work. I hope you catch whoever did this."

"I'll be in touch if I have more questions," I said.

"I'll do everything I can to help you. Come along, Nimbus. We'll find Cythera, then it's straight to bed for us."

"Good luck with that." The angels Cythera had sent were already gone, and I had little hope of Cythera or Bertoli returning to see how things were going. I was solving this murder without their help.

Chapter 5

Clues and suspects

My head jerked off the pillow, and I saw the empty spot where Zandra should have been resting. Although this bed was comfortable, and I had all the space I could desire and my pillow of choice, I'd give it all up to have Zandra back, snoring beside me, her hair a tangled bird's nest around her head. This basement wasn't the same without her, and neither was I.

I stretched and jumped off the bed. I needed to focus on finding my witch, not solving a murder. But every avenue I'd tried had failed. At least this murder felt like I could get my claws into it and grill some suspects.

I headed up the basement steps and into the kitchen. Sage was sprawled on the prickly mat by the back door, her fur unwashed and her eyes crusty with sleep.

She barely lifted her head to acknowledge me. "I survived the night."

"I'm happy you did," I said.

"I wish I hadn't. All hope is lost."

I gently dabbed her with a paw. "Pull yourself together. We have a mission to focus on."

"I refuse to get involved in one of your stupid kitten impossible missions," Sage said. "It'll end in disaster for me. Remember, I have experience."

"Disasters never happen on my missions. Especially not to you."

"Only because I refuse to take part in them."

"And by doing so, you miss out on the fun."

"I've heard what goes on from the others. You insist on playing the heroine, and then chaos ensues, usually whacking into everyone else."

"There's only ever a dash of chaos." I nudged Sage again when she shut her eyes. "We must do this. Angel Force is useless, so we're in charge of finding out what happened to Azureus."

"Why bother?" Sage asked. "It's not as if we knew him."

"That's hardly the attitude," I said. "We need Crimson Cove safe and back to normal for when Zandra and Vorana come home."

"Remind me again, when is that happening?" Sage flopped onto her side and heaved out a sigh. "We've tried everything to get them back. Nothing works. And I don't work without Vorana with me. I feel stodgy and slow."

"You may be misshapen without her, but you're doing fine." I settled on the edge of the prickly mat. It did have a certain delightful quality under paw.

"I'm not fine! I'm giving up. As of today, I'm going on a hunger strike. I'm not eating until Vorana comes home. And if she doesn't..." The rest was left unsaid, but I understood the lingering warning.

"None of that. When Vorana returns, she won't want you an emaciated mess that needs caring for. You have to show her how robust you are."

"I'm not robust. And I miss being carried in my papoose." Sage slid me some side-eye. "Do you really think Zandra and Vorana will come home?"

"They're coming back. I'm sure of it. Whatever is going on, it's out of their control and therefore ours. As frustrating as the situation is, we need to focus on what we can control."

"Which is nothing!"

"We focus on keeping our heads up and solving this murder. Finding a killer gives us a useful purpose."

"I still don't get why you can't leave it to Angel Force," Sage said. "Given the mood Cythera is in, she won't want us poking around and making her look like an idiot when we find the killer."

"She handed me the case. And you saw what the angels were like yesterday. They're uninterested in figuring out this crime. They disturbed evidence, abandoned the crime scene, and forgot the body. I had to go back and move Azureus to the morgue. It was as if they'd forgotten they're in charge of law and order."

Sage grunted out her displeasure then gave a small nod. "They have been acting strangely. Just like everybody else."

"Almost everybody else," I said. "We're fine."

"Why?"

"Why what?"

"Why do we seem normal when everyone else is so altered and odd?" Sage lifted herself up and shook out her clumpy fur. "Something is spreading through Crimson Cove and making people act strangely, but it's ignoring us."

"If that's the case, I'm happy it is," I said. "If our heads were as befuddled as everybody else's, we'd have no interest in finding our lost witches or solving this crime. Zandra and Vorana will be so proud of us if we figure out this mystery. Not just the murder, but why Crimson Cove has been tainted by strangeness."

"I'm not so sure about that," Sage said. "After all, Zandra stole your magic stones."

"There's no evidence of that."

"Show me the stones."

I quietly hissed at her. "If Zandra took them, it was a mistake. She must have grabbed them when she was hurrying to pack." At least, I hoped that was the truth. If Zandra knew how much power was in those stones and used it, it wouldn't end well for her. Or me. "Let's team up and do this together. Two fluffy heads are better than one."

"You've not seen the inside of my head," Sage groused. "But you won't leave me alone until I agree to help, will you?"

"Sadly for you, no. We're partners. We'll solve Azureus's murder and figure out what's gone wrong with Crimson Cove. One mystery at a time."

Sage closed her eyes. "What do I have to do?"

"Forage for breakfast in the pantry. Then you need to groom, since you smell like a decaying toad. After that, we'll go to Angel Force and see if they've made progress overnight."

"Some hope of that," Sage said.

"I always have hope. Even if it's only a tiny amount. Hope keeps me going."

Half an hour later, we were on the road. Literally trotting along the center of the street. It was quiet, but it was early, so I didn't expect to see many people around. We arrived at Angel Force to find the main doors locked.

"They should be open," Sage said. "Don't they always have at least one angel on duty in case of an emergency?"

I rested my front paws on a window ledge and peered through. "There are no signs of life inside. And you're right. An angel always stays behind when the others are out on calls."

"They're probably still in bed after partying at the toadstool event," Sage said.

"Mushroom festival." Angel Force may not always be effective at solving crimes, but they stick to the rules. At least, they used to. "Let's try around the back. A window may have been left open, so we can get in that way."

We tested all the doors and windows, but there was no way in. And every time we looked inside, there was no movement. The angels had deserted their posts.

"We have to get in," I said. "I want to examine Azureus's body, and we need to check on Adrienne and Joel. I only glimpsed them last night after everything that happened, and I want to make sure the angels are looking after them properly. If no angel has been in all night, they'll be starving."

"Which will make them even meaner. I'll get us inside. Stand back." Sage pressed a paw to the back door we stood beside. It quivered under her magic and imploded, leaving behind a scatter of wood chips and ash.

"Impressive. Where did you learn that trick?"

"I'm channeling my inner despair," Sage said. "I have an endless supply. You can have some if you like."

"You keep your despair to yourself." Even though I was putting on a brave face, there was a part of me that wanted to curl up into a ball and never move again. I still had my connection to Zandra, but without her by my side, everything felt wrong. But I was determined not to let it beat me. And I refused to consider the possibility I may never see her again.

"We'll go to the cells first," I said. "Then we'll look at Azureus's body."

As soon as we got into the cell corridor, snarls and growls filled the air. Adrienne and Joel were awake.

"At least they're still alive," Sage muttered. "Well, as alive as ghouls can be."

"And still angry." I stopped outside the cell they were in. Adrienne and Joel rampaged about, snarling and snapping at nothing in particular, grabbing at imaginary things in front of them and chewing as if they were eating something.

"Greetings," I said.

Their heads whipped around, and they lunged. The cell bars and magic wards prevented them from touching us, and they bounced harmlessly off the magic.

"I hope you had a restful night," I said. "Although if you've been pacing like that for hours, you must be exhausted."

Adrienne's normally placid face contorted with uncontrolled rage. She hissed and spat at us for several seconds. It seemed she'd lost the power of speech.

"They're hungry," Sage said.

"Check the fridge in the kitchen and bring back any meat you can find. Cooked or raw, it doesn't matter. Look in the freezer box, too."

Sage turned and trudged away.

"Adrienne, I know this is hard for you, but you must focus to get back your control. Cythera wants to destroy you because of your bad behavior in the woods, and you don't want that. Focus on coming back to me. I know you're in there."

My pleas fell on unlistening ears as she attempted to reach me again with her clawed fingers, drooling at the prospect of taking a chunk out of my purrfect form.

Sage returned a moment later with an unopened packet of ham. I sliced it open with my claws and tossed the contents into the cell. Adrienne and Joel devoured it with an excess of slurping and growling.

"The food hasn't made them any happier," Sage said, keeping a safe distance from the cell. "We should have kept it for ourselves. It was still in date. And it had been smoked."

"I thought you were considering a hunger strike?"

She huffed at me. "It was just an idea, and that ham smelled delicious."

"We can grab ham for ourselves later." I studied the snappy ghouls. "I think if they chewed on everybody in town, they'd still be full of rage. Let's visit the morgue and see what we can learn from Azureus's body."

We left the furious, snarling ghouls and walked the short distance to the morgue.

"I'm not looking at a corpse," Sage said. "I'll stand by the door as a show of support, but you have to deal with the gross bits."

I could understand my grumpy friend's caution. I never enjoyed dealing with the dead, but it was necessary to study the flesh to find the clues. After a quick examination of Azureus's body and finding no other injuries, it was clear the method of death was strangulation.

I hopped off the gurney and wiped my murder mittens on a clean cloth. "In a town surrounded by powerful magic users, it's an odd way to kill someone. Whoever did it would have needed to be close to strangle Azureus."

"Maybe they wanted to look him in the eye so he knew who was taking his life," Sage said.

"Perhaps. Or they saw the perfect opportunity but didn't have their magic prepared."

"Roland mentioned Gilly Piper had a problem with Azureus."

"They were professional rivals. Although their disputes didn't strike me as the kind of thing they'd kill each other over. Arguments over fungus classification can't get that heated. Gilly is worth talking to, though."

"Do you think Angel Force allowed the festival to continue?" Sage was happy to leave the morgue and follow me into the empty open-plan office.

"I have a feeling they couldn't care less about it," I said. "Perhaps Cythera even encouraged it so she could continue eating truffles. Let's head over there and see what's going on. It started at nine, so will already be in full swing."

"If the festival's been called off, Gilly is probably staying in a local hotel, so we can try those," Sage said.

I gently head-butted her as a show of affection. "I told you helping solve a murder would cheer you up."

"Yeah, yeah. Whatever you say. But I'm still not cheerful. Let's get this over with so I can go back to sleep and dream about ham and Vorana."

As we grew closer to the festival site, the music and crowds revealed it was very much on and seemed even bigger than yesterday. We stopped by the events board to see what fungi fun was on the schedule for today.

"That's the guy we're looking for." Sage dabbed a paw on the board. "Gilly is giving the first demonstration of the day about the relaxing properties of fungi. It finishes in ten minutes. If we hurry, we can catch him before he leaves."

"Then let's make haste."

The marquee where Gilly was demonstrating was packed, so we had to sneak in under the fabric and conceal ourselves at the back as he wound up his talk. Everyone raucously applauded, and Gilly spent twenty minutes shaking hands and signing autographs.

The second I saw an opportunity, I dashed out and stood in front of him. "Greetings! We're expert consultants hired by Angel Force. I'm Juno, and this is Sage."

Gilly nodded. "Welcome. Did you enjoy my talk?"

"Very much. Although we only caught the end of it. I don't know if you remember me. We met on the first evening of the festival."

Gilly peered at me. "Of course. You were asking about our mushroom mage."

"Excellent memory." I stepped out of the way as an eager fan begged for an autograph on her embroidered apron. "I won't waste your time. I see you're a busy man."

"Run off my feet dealing with my fans." He smiled tightly. "You know how it is."

"I do! It's wonderful to have so many admirers."

His forehead wrinkled as if he was working out if I was being sarcastic or overly nice. "Did you want something?"

"I'm sure you've heard about Azureus's sad demise."

"Oh! That's what you're looking into?" Gilly paused to sign another autograph.

"It's a serious business that requires the best and the brightest on the case," I said. "You mentioned not approving of Azureus's meteoric rise to fungi fame. Could you tell me more about that?"

Gilly sniffed. "Not really. I'm sorry he's dead, but I had no respect for the man."

"Why would that be?" I asked.

"There are rumors, and even some evidence, to suggest Azureus used a ghostwriter for his scholarly articles. He also published three books that weren't written by him."

"How do you know that?" Sage asked.

"Because I questioned him extensively on the contents of each book and his articles. Azureus fumbled most of the answers and was unable to supply me with the information he allegedly wrote. The man was a scammer. He was an embarrassment to our community."

"Did you confront him with your beliefs?" I asked.

Gilly gathered his papers and satchel from a nearby table. "I despise people pretending to be something they aren't. Azureus pretended he had this natural talent and affinity with fungi, but he was a fraud."

I followed Gilly as he marched about, collecting his things. "What was your proof of that?"

"I looked at his early work. Essays, short articles, that kind of thing, and compared them to his most recent books. The style was completely different. Much better, too. He had someone working for him. An expert in fungi. They'd need to be loyal and most likely well-paid to hold their tongue and not share the secret. Azureus made a fortune from his books, so he could pay well to ensure his dirty little scam didn't escape and ruin his golden boy reputation."

"I never realized there was so much interest in fungi," I said.

"You'd be surprised. Now, if that's all, I need to get ready for my next presentation."

"One more thing," I said. "What were you doing yesterday evening around nine pm?"

Gilly hesitated. "Why do you want to know?"

"You've admitted to not liking Azureus, and now he's dead. And as I'm sure you've heard, the death wasn't an accident."

"I... Yes, I heard that. Roland found Azureus, didn't he? That had nothing to do with me," Gilly said.

"You were jealous of Azureus's success?" Sage asked. "Some would say that's a motive."

"Of course it's not." Gilly slung the satchel over his shoulder. "I didn't appreciate the way he went about his business, but anyone who has a passion for fungi has a place in my world."

"So, where were you last night?" I asked.

Gilly sighed. "If you must know, I was communing with our Grand Mushroom Mage. I like to unwind with a long meditation session. Kinoko invited me to join him and, of course, I agreed. He does the best meditation practices. Now, I must go." He dashed off.

"Meditation rather than murder," Sage said. "What do you think about him?"

"I think Gilly Piper is self-important and not telling the whole truth," I said. "Let's find this Grand Mushroom Mage and see what words of mushroomy, mystical wisdom he can impart."

Chapter 6

Moldy facts

"Everyone has fungus on them. It may be in between your toes, inside your ears, or nestled in a groin crevice, but we share our lives with fungi. It's a truly wonderful partnership." The Grand Mushroom Mage, Kinoko Sporeleigh, spread his arms wide, revealing his long brown speckled batwing cloak to his adoring audience, his gray beard resting on his waistband.

"I feel queasy," Sage muttered.

I nodded, my booping snooter crinkled as I checked my groin folds for unwanted fungus, while keeping an eye on the excitable crowd in the marquee we'd squeezed ourselves into so we could speak to Kinoko.

"There's no need to fear the fungi," Kinoko said. "For centuries, it was misunderstood or ignored while it was busy weaving its magic upon us all, finding friendly hosts and those with open minds who were willing to accept how incredible fungi truly are."

"Friends of the fungi!" the crowd chanted.

I whipped my tail neatly around my front paws to avoid it being trodden on as the crowd in the marquee kept chanting, and I nudged Sage. "If Kinoko blows any more hot air, we'll all end up with a yeast infection. The guy loves the sound of his own voice."

"Fungi aren't yeast, are they?" Sage rubbed an ear on the floor. "He's been talking for over an hour, and I can barely keep my eyes open. It's so hot in here."

"A perfectly moist environment for the fungi to creep into folds and damp places it shouldn't." I double-checked my groin.

Several people shushed us before turning their attention back to Kinoko and hollering the friends of the fungi chant. It was repeated every ten minutes or so. I'd also spotted numerous T-shirts with the slogan on them. There was probably a stall selling mugs and towels with the words on them, too.

"I do not have a partnership with any kind of mushroom, toadstool, or gross fungi spore," Sage whispered. "This guy is off his rocker if he thinks we all adore mold. Who believes this insanity?"

"Everyone in here," I said. "They love Kinoko."

"More like they love the free mushroom favors his assistants are handing out. They're most likely spiked with mind-altering ingredients."

"Don't eat any," I said. "We need clear heads to focus on this mystery."

"They're making the place smell worse than my fur," Sage said. "I wouldn't eat them if I was starving."

"If you can't respect the Grand Mushroom Mage, you'll have to leave," a sharp-faced woman said to us. "I've been waiting to hear him speak for a year. Show some respect."

"My apologies," I murmured. "We're new to the world of fungal fantasies."

"Then keep your mouth shut and listen. You might learn something." She returned her attention to Kinoko and lifted her hands in the air.

"Before I end this enchanting gathering, I'd like to spend a moment remembering a recently fallen colleague, lost while serving the fungi," Kinoko said. "Azureus Stool was an incredible individual with a deep devotion to all things fungi. He was a devout servant and a loyal follower. Please, raise your candles, and we'll say a silent prayer for Azureus."

I was astonished to see the crowd whip out small mushroom-shaped candles, which they lit. They must have been given out to people as they arrived in the marquee before the talk started. The candles were held aloft, and everyone swayed as they closed their eyes and offered up a prayer.

"Kinoko is putting on an act." Sage's nose was pressed up against my ear, so she wouldn't be overheard badmouthing the mage. "He's pretending to be sad so the finger of guilt doesn't get pointed at him."

"He must have planned this showy display. How did he get those mushroom candles so quickly?" I whispered.

"They're part of his merchandise. I saw some on a stall."

"We'll know if he's hiding something when he tells us his alibi," I said. "But if Kinoko was with Gilly, neither of them could have murdered Azureus."

The silent praying ended, and the candles were lowered. Rather than the crowd leaving, they surged forward to speak to Kinoko. Unless we wanted to get trodden on and our tails damaged, we had no choice but to wait at the back of the marquee until the fan crush eased.

After twenty minutes of watching Kinoko shake hands, sign autographs, and make friendly chitchat, we were able to get close enough to catch his attention.

He looked down at us, deep lines lacing around his eyes and mouth. His gaze settled on Sage and her harness as he tucked a long string of beads under his cloak. "If you've come for healing, I'm the wrong mage to consult. Of course, I'm happy to see if there's anything I can do. Fungi is a friend to all. Its healing powers are extraordinary." Without Sage's permission, he settled his hand on her rump.

She hissed at him and backed away. "I know I can't be healed. I made peace with that a long time ago. Keep your hands to yourself."

Kinoko looked mildly surprised, but a benign smile crossed his face. "As you wish. And as I feared, that is a complicated injury. Far beyond my healing skills."

I stepped in before Sage's hissing grew any fiercer. "Greetings! We're not here about Sage. She's perfectly capable in her harness."

"Of course. So... why are you here? Do you have something for me to autograph?"

"We have questions about Azureus," I said. "We're investigating his death."

"Ah! My lost companion. It's a tragedy what happened to him. I was pleased to bring everyone together to remember him."

"How did you hear about his death?" I asked.

"Most people have been talking about it since the festival opened this morning," he said. "Although an assistant passed on the news late last night, just before I retired. It took me time to get to sleep as I recalled happy memories with Azureus. You say you're investigating?"

"Angel Force has their hands full, so we've stepped in," I said. "We're fully experienced and qualified to solve the most puzzling crime."

Kinoko lifted an eyebrow. "I'm glad to hear it. Azureus deserves the best."

"So you won't mind answering a few questions?" I asked. "We need to get a clear picture of what happened last night."

Kinoko twisted his beard around one hand. "I'll answer your questions if you answer mine."

"We can't disclose information about an active investigation," I said, "but I'm open to negotiation."

"I only have one question," Kinoko said. "When may I collect Azureus's body?"

"His body won't be released for some time," I said. "Not until we know what happened to him and who killed him. And even then, his family will need to be consulted. They have rights."

Kinoko's nostrils flared. "I heard his death wasn't an accident. Someone mentioned strangulation. Is that correct?"

"Your connections are well-informed," I said. "Who gave you that information?"

"The event organizer, Roland Moldsworth. He said he found Azureus. The unfortunate fellow was beside himself. I gave him several mushroom favors to calm him. They do wonders for the nerves. Would you like some?"

"We'll pass," I said. "What do you want with Azureus's body? Are you family?"

"No, we're not related, but we follow the same path once we die."

"What path is that?" Sage asked.

"To continue our devotion to the fungi," Kinoko said, "we allow our bodies to be used as fertilizer for a rare and powerful crop of mushrooms that are grown in a secret location. Only a select few know where that location is. If the wrong people get their hands on that crop, it would be disastrous."

Sage snorted her surprise. "You're using Azureus to feed a mushroom crop?"

"Naturally. Nature is always hungry. And this way, it means he lives forever," Kinoko said. "Azureus's nutrients will fertilize the mushrooms, and then we use the rare fungi for spells, powders, mushroom favors. All sorts of delicious things."

"You're telling me there are dead bodies in those free mushroom favors you've been giving out to everybody?" Sage wrinkled her nose. "Do they know what they're chewing on?"

"Only in the purest sense," Kinoko said. "We don't chop up fingers and put them in the favors. The bodies are buried and left to decompose naturally. Their nutrients enhance the soil, which in turn feeds the mushroom crop. The mushrooms absorb the nutrients. Azureus is reborn into the thing he adored the most. It's poetic. It's how it should be. Poetry in fungi."

"It's unusual, but I've heard of similar rituals in certain religions," I said.

"I look forward to my time. But the burial must happen within the first week of death. It's when Azureus's energy is most vibrant and will benefit the fungi." Kinoko leaned down. "Are you sure you can't tell me when his body will be released? I can pay."

"We have more work to do," I said. "And since Azureus was strangled, we're searching for a killer. That could take time."

"How long?"

"It depends how cooperative people are."

"That is unfortunate. I hoped to fulfil Azureus's last wishes." Kinoko tucked his hands into his long sleeves. "Have you had any success in finding out who lost their way and committed such a terrible thing?"

"We've just started the investigation," I said. "What was your opinion of Azureus?"

"He was remarkable. We shared a mutual respect for each other's work."

"No, you didn't," Sage said.

"What was that?" Kinoko took a step back.

"You didn't respect Azureus. I read an article about your messy public feud. I knew I recognized you from somewhere, but it wasn't until I got up close that I remembered from where."

"Where do you know Kinoko from?" I asked.

"Vorana recently subscribed to a weekly mushroom magazine. I couldn't figure out why the sudden interest, but I assumed she wanted inspiration for cooking. Since she's been gone, I've been catching up on my reading. She left the latest magazine on the kitchen table, and I've been looking through it. There was a center-page article all about a feud between Azureus and Kinoko. There was even a color photograph of them arguing."

"That's the media hyping up nothing," Kinoko said. "They needed a story, so they made one up."

"You had no disagreement with Azureus?" I asked.

Kinoko opened his mouth, but Sage beat him to it. "The article said Kinoko was unhappy because Azureus secured a top speaking spot at a prestigious conference abroad. Is that true?"

"I'm booked for so many events that I barely remember where I've been and where I'm going." Kinoko adjusted his bell sleeves. "Besides, my people do all the bookings. I simply turn up and share the mushroomy love."

"Are your memory problems because you've eaten too many extra special mushroom favors?" I asked.

"My memory is excellent. Fungi only enhances. It never takes away."

I didn't believe that. Not having witnessed so many hyped up, glassy-eyed festival goers wandering around. "We're learning that the world of fungi experts is full of rivalry. Some may say jealousy. Were you jealous of Azureus's success?"

"Look around you," Kinoko said. "My talk was sold out. There are fans waiting to speak to me, and my diary is full for eighteen months. I have nothing to be jealous of. If anything, Azureus should have been envious of me. But he wasn't. Yes, occasionally, we clashed over a difference of opinion in relation to our profession, but we were forging our own paths. I had no issue with him."

"You don't seem saddened by his death," I said. "I suppose, with Azureus gone, it means a problem has been removed."

"He was never a problem for me. And I'm a professional. If I have tears to shed, they happen behind closed doors. My fans need me. I'm their anchor and a source of refuge. If I'm seen falling apart, what will happen to them?"

"They'll see an individual having genuine feelings and empathize with your struggle," I said. "It's not a weakness to show you're upset. But I don't think you are. Perhaps you'll be celebrating with Gilly tonight because you've gotten rid of a thorn in your side."

"I'd never celebrate a murder." Kinoko's calm veneer had hardened like varnish. "It wounds me that you say such a thing. I spread love and benevolence within the community. We get passionate about our cause and tempers fray, but if you don't have a passion for something, you don't have a purpose."

"Passion can lead to impulsive behavior." I squinted at Kinoko. Just like Sage, I wasn't buying his benign mage act.

Kinoko sensed my suspicion. "If I shed a tear, will you leave me alone?"

"We're almost finished," I said. "Tell us what you were doing at the end of the festival's first night. We're gathering information about people's movements to find out what happened during Azureus's last moments."

"Is that your way of finding out if I had an opportunity to kill him?" Kinoko asked.

"I was attempting to be discreet, but yes, we'd like your alibi." His evasive nature irked me. I had far less patience when Zandra wasn't by my side.

Kinoko's smile was tinged with smugness. "I was in another dimension. Many dimensions, in fact."

"What does that mean?" Sage asked.

"There are certain types of fungi that move you into different worlds. You cross the barrier and discover a whole new space to explore." Kinoko pointed at the last of the mushroom favors passing us on a serving tray. "Try them and see for yourself. These offerings aren't as potent, but the effects will give you an idea."

I shook my head. We were going nowhere near his mind-altering fungi.

"Were you traveling alone?" Sage asked.

"No, I never do interdimensional meditation alone. Sometimes it's tempting to remain there, and if you lose your way, you become stuck," Kinoko said. "I was with Gilly Piper. Do you know him?"

"We've met," I said. "Where did you do this interdimensional meditation?"

"I have a studio set up close by. My assistants call it a glamping unit. It's essentially a huge tent with all my provisions. I prefer to camp among the common people. They appreciate it. The everyday folk rarely get the privilege to mingle with people such as myself."

"I'm sure it brings joy to their hearts," I said. "How long did the meditation go on?"

"That's the thing about interdimensional meditative practices. Time has little meaning. You can slip from one dimension to another in the blink of an eye, but sometimes it takes hours. One never knows where the fungi will take you."

"Measure it in our time," I snapped. "We have a murder to solve."

Kinoko's smile slipped. "My last talk finished at eight pm. Gilly was in the crowd, and he joined me. We spoke to the fans and then walked back to my glamping unit. It took longer than usual because we kept being stopped and asked for autographs or photographs. Such is the life of a star."

"Sounds terrible," Sage said. She meant it. Sage wasn't a people person, unless that person was Vorana.

"It is taxing, but you must give back to the common people. We arrived back at the tent around eight-thirty and began the session straightaway. I always have my batch of meditative interdimensional dried truffles ready to go. It's essential to have a substantial wind-down after such a trying evening."

"The common people can be wearing," I said.

"They are! I'm blessed to use methods that liberate me from the everyday drudge that is life for so many. Now, I must leave you. The fans wait for no mage, and this mage is always popular." Kinoko reached out and pressed the tip of his finger to our heads in turn. "A blessing from me to you. May your endeavors to find out what happened to Azureus be successful." He drifted off and returned to a group of adoring fans.

"I feel so much happier now I've been blessed by that idiot," Sage said.

"I wasn't charmed by him either, but he knows how to work a crowd." My attention was on the dozens of people who held out books and posters to be signed or begged for selfies with Kinoko. "I don't see the allure."

"Look into their eyes, and you'll see dilated pupils. He's got them hooked on his mushroom favors. There's no mystery about why they want to be his best friend. They want a piece of the mushroom action. It's just a bunch of hippies getting high and playing at being cool, man."

"It's not illegal to use mushrooms to relax," I said. "Angel Force would never have allowed the festival to go ahead if the organizers supplied unethical substances."

"You sure about that? After how weird they've been?" Sage stamped a paw. "Cythera probably didn't even check who Roland invited to this spaced-out chaos."

"You have a point. The angels are only keen on sampling the free mushroom treats rather than figuring out who strangled Azureus."

Sage shuffled closer as she yawned. "What do we do now?"

"Search for more suspects," I said.

"Shouldn't we look for our witches? It's been hours since I cast a fresh location spell for Vorana." She yawned again.

"We are looking for them! We have location spells active, alerts out everywhere, and I test my magic bond all the time."

"Is Zandra testing your bond?" Sage asked. "I keep tugging on my link with Vorana, but she doesn't respond. It's there, but she's ignoring me."

"I'm sure they want to respond, but maybe they can't. Whatever has happened to them means they've lost touch with what matters. Our witches wouldn't desert us unless something had gone horribly wrong. We'll get them back."

"If we're not looking for Zandra and Vorana, we should sleep," Sage said. "All this peopling is exhausting."

"It's not just that. We're burning through our magic with all this searching. Keeping spells active all day and night is wearing."

"I'd burn up every spell I had and give it all away if it meant I got Vorana back."

I patted my tired friend's head. "You sleep. I'm visiting Roland and Nimbus."

Chapter 7

The mystery deepens

I knocked and peered, peered and knocked, but Roland and Nimbus weren't home. I even checked round the back of the house, but everything was locked, and there were no signs of occupation. Had Roland returned to the festival? The man had barely been able to stand after the shock of almost stepping on a corpse.

But there was no other explanation for where he could be. Roland had been obsessed with the mushroom festival ever since he'd moved to Crimson Cove. Why let one little murder spoil such a joy-filled event? This festival was probably the highlight of his year. Maybe the decade. Possibly his life!

I hurried away from his house and headed back to the festival. Sage had wandered off to Vorana's for a long nap, and although I'd been tempted to join her, the business of murder solving waited for no velvet paw.

Having such a bustling event in town complicated this mystery and opened the door to a host of possible suspects. What if Azureus annoyed a mushroom-fogged stranger, and they strangled him? If they were passing through Crimson Cove, there'd be zero chance of finding them, and I'd be left with an unsolved crime and a body that was due to become mushroom compost.

As I drew closer to the festival, I discovered even more people had arrived. Word must have spread that there'd been a murder on the first day. A sniff of death and scandal always encouraged curious onlookers to visit and gossip. Sometimes, that gossip led to useful information. But all this noise and people milling about was a problem I could do without. I should insist Angel Force close the event and send everybody home, but given the odd mood the angels were in, I'd be shouting into the dark and getting batted on the head with a heavy feathered wing for making such a suggestion.

It took some searching and asking around, but I eventually discovered Roland and Nimbus talking with a petite goth stallholder, who sold everything as long as it came in black or gray. I even spotted several stuffed toy vampire cat bat hybrids with striped fur.

Nimbus saw me lingering and growled a warning for me to shove off.

"Greetings! I'm surprised to see you both here," I said, interrupting Roland's conversation. "I thought you'd need a few days in bed to recover."

Roland glanced my way. He held up a finger, finished his conversation, and scurried toward me. "Everyone expects the festival to go ahead, and I can't disappoint all these people."

"Are you sure it's a good idea to keep things running? There's still a killer to find."

Roland gently shushed me and moved us to a quieter spot beside a marquee. "Sorry. I don't mean to be bossy, but I don't want to upset anybody if they overhear our conversation."

"If my suspicions are correct, the increased number of visitors today is because of the body. Some people have morbid hobbies," I said.

Roland scrubbed his chin. "You could be right. Although don't underestimate the passion for fungi. And I know some say it's distasteful to carry on after what happened, but as I said yesterday, this is what Azureus would want. He loved a festival, and he was so passionate about fungi."

"So I keep hearing," I said. "Do you have a moment to talk?"

"No moments to spare," Nimbus said. "Not even seconds. Too busy, we are. Chaos, it is."

"I like to think of it as organized chaos," Roland said as he gently patted Nimbus. "A few people overindulged yesterday, but generally, it was a great success."

"Apart from the murder," I said.

Roland's smile faded, and his lower jaw wobbled. "Yes! I keep trying not to think about it, but then it springs to the front of my thoughts."

"You need to think about it," I said. "Because Azureus's death was no accident."

"Oh! Oh, dear. You're right. Am I being selfish?" Tears glazed Roland's eyes.

"Away you go," Nimbus said on a hiss. "Not wanted, you are. Troublemaker."

"I'm not here to cause trouble, but I will make sure justice is done," I said.

Nimbus growled fiercely until Roland calmed her.

"I... I want to help in any way I can," Roland said. "I even made sure the area where Azureus's body was found was blocked off, so no one could walk through it. I don't know if that was any help. I suppose you found everything you needed last night."

"That's the trouble. We found very little at the scene to solve this crime," I said. "Azureus was strangled, but his killer must have taken the murder weapon with them."

"That's unhelpful." Roland looked down at the notepad he held. "I wish I could be more useful, but I've got a huge list of tasks to get through. I had a team of volunteers, but they keep wandering off, so it's only Nimbus and me looking after things."

"But you can help me." I tamped down my frustration. "I need to know everything that happened in the lead-up to you finding Azureus's body."

"There's nothing to tell." Roland glanced toward raucous laughter, which was coming from a marquee. Angel Force were in there having a party. Drinking and eating and acting as if they didn't have a care in the world. I'd have words with them as soon as I was done with Roland and Nimbus.

"Too busy for this furry and her questions," Nimbus said.

"Make time for me," I said. "As you can see, the angels are otherwise occupied. I'm leading this investigation, and I will get to the bottom of what happened to Azureus."

"Of course. Of course. Sorry. We can spare Juno time," Roland said.

"Thank you." I refused to engage in a hissing contest with Nimbus, no matter how tempting it was.

"I knew Azureus," Roland said. "I'm an enthusiastic amateur, but I like to think I had his respect."

"Would you say you were friends?" I asked.

"Acquaintances. Azureus's star shone brightly, and he had an enormous fan base. I could never hope to become that popular. Besides, I'd find it too overwhelming. I like the quiet of fungi foraging. It's peaceful. Just me, Nimbus, and nature. Nothing beats it."

"That sounds blissful," I said. "Azureus and Kinoko seem to have a similar level of fame. When I spoke to Kinoko, he had fans clamoring for his attention."

"Our mage is wise, powerful, and well-liked. But his position comes with great responsibility. It would be too much for me to manage, but I heard a rumor Azureus was next in line for that position," Roland said. "As Grand Mushroom Mage, you preside over all things magically fungi-related. It's a coveted position. Not by me, of course. Too many public events and important decisions to make for my liking. When I'm under pressure, I can't make any decisions and get an upset stomach."

"You shouldn't put yourself down," I said. "You're doing a great job of handling this event without much support."

"So far, but you never know when trouble is lurking around the corner. I wouldn't want to be the mage. Far too stressful."

"How is the vacancy filled?" I asked. "Does the current mage serve a particular length of time and then step down?"

"Provided they get voted in every five years, they stay in the role for as long as they desire. The longest the role has been filled by the same person is sixty years."

That was useful information. Kinoko had told me he'd been inter-dimensionally meditating with Gilly at the time of the murder, but perhaps he'd felt threatened by Azureus's rising star and was concerned his role as Grand Mushroom Mage was vulnerable to attack. Would he have had an opportunity to sneak off and destroy his competition?

"Let's go back to yesterday evening," I said. "You told me you were tidying at the end of the festival and making sure the stallholders were happy."

"That's right." Roland lifted his notepad. "I keep a record of everything I need to do and tick it off as I go. I like to keep organized. I'd been to nearly all the stalls, checking behind each one to ensure everything was tidy for the next day. That's when I found Azureus's body."

"How long were you there before I arrived?" I asked.

"Ten seconds at the most. I found him, couldn't believe my eyes, then cried out for help. You were the first on the scene," Roland said.

"And you're sure you didn't see anyone running away?"

"No. There was no one."

"What about anyone acting furtively around Azureus during the day? Anything you saw or heard could be helpful to figuring out who did this."

Roland considered the question then shook his head. "It all happened so fast. I could have missed something. To begin with, I thought Azureus was asleep, but it was such a strange place to take a nap. Then I saw the marks around his neck. That's when I realized something terrible had happened to him."

There was more over-the-top laughter from the marquee Angel Force was inhabiting. I pressed down my irritation. They should be doing this, not me. I wanted to be looking for Zandra and Vorana, not mopping up the aftermath of someone's cruelty.

"I... err... Have you talked to Gilly Piper yet?" Roland asked. "I mentioned to you that they weren't keen on each other."

"I have. It wasn't him. He was with Kinoko. They were conducting interdimensional meditation to wind down after the festival."

"Oh! I didn't realize they were that close," Roland said. "That's a sacred act. You only travel with those you implicitly trust."

"They don't like each other?"

"It's not that." Roland glanced around. "But Gilly likes to gossip and talk about people behind their backs. It made him unpopular in some circles."

"Gilly had an air of snideness about him," I said. "And he has an overly large amount of self-esteem. A healthy ego is no bad thing, but when it gets too large, it needs to be popped. Nobody is that perfect."

"Certainly not me," Roland said. "You could fit my ego into an egg cup."

"Big gross ego, he has," Nimbus said. "Nasty little man. Like Gilly, we do not."

"Gilly does his best," Roland said. "But he was pressing our main committee to have Azureus's license taken away, so he couldn't legally hunt for new fungi. Ultimately, that decision would have been made by Kinoko."

"Could Gilly have convinced Kinoko to remove Azureus's license?" I asked.

"I don't know for certain. Maybe. They must be close if they're meditating together," Roland said. "As I've mentioned, I don't travel along the same lofty paths of mushroomy esteem, but I wouldn't be surprised if Kinoko was considering it. Azureus's expertise came from an unconventional route."

"He was untrained," I said.

"Self-taught," Roland corrected. "The usual path to becoming an expert and having an opportunity to serve as the Grand Mushroom Mage requires a decade of extensive study. You must also produce academic papers and at least one non-fiction book. And you must have taught in an area of specialty for at least twenty years."

"Azureus never studied at a conventional university?" I asked.

"No, but he was awarded three honorary degrees last year. He had his own methods of gaining knowledge. And he knew the subject inside and out," Roland said. "He was raised in a traveling community, and they spent a lot of time living on the edges of forests, which gave Azureus ample opportunity to get hands-on experience with finding fungi and working with it."

"When I spoke to Gilly, he wasn't impressed by Azureus's training," I said.

"I've no doubt about that. It's expensive to train in this industry. Most students get into debt to gain their qualifications. It's no wonder many resent Azureus for getting a free education and being willingly accepted into the community."

"Accepted by most," I said.

Roland nodded. "There are always a few who don't approve of difference."

"That could be a motive for wanting him dead," I said.

"I wondered about that, which was why I suggested Gilly. But if Gilly was with Kinoko, then it couldn't have been him." Roland scratched his forehead. "I'm no expert, so I'll leave the crime solving up to you and Angel Force."

"I'm surprised you mentioned Kinoko was considering taking Azureus's license away," I said. "When I spoke to him, Kinoko said he respected Azureus. Was he lying to me? There have been reports in the media about a feud between them."

Roland's eyes widened, and he vigorously shook his head. "I'd never suggest such a thing of our Grand Mushroom Mage. He's honorable and benevolent."

"In on it together, they were," Nimbus said. "Both mage and the ego gossip. They killed Azureus."

"Hush now, Nimbus. Don't say things like that," Roland cautioned.

"Do you have any proof to back up that accusation?" I asked Nimbus.

"Nasty little men," Nimbus said. "Grasping. Greedy. Always want more."

"It's not nice to say unkind words about people," Roland said. "Everyone tries their best. And you're only annoyed with them because they bought the last tray of chocolate fudge truffles, and you were looking forward to those."

Nimbus grumbled her agreement. "Best is sometimes a disaster. Embarrassing behavior, it can be. Their best, my worst. Shameful. Greedy truffle snufflers."

"Please excuse Nimbus," Roland said. "She's tired. We had a long day yesterday, and she spent much of last night patrolling because she was worried the killer might strike again."

"Do you think they'll come after you?" I asked.

"No! Why would they? I'm a small, harmless toadstool in the grand scheme of fungi education and exploration. Barely anyone knows me. But you know how our familiars can be. Well, sorry, of course, you're a familiar. But you must be protective of your witch when she's in danger."

"I always look out for Zandra, even though she doesn't need it." I ignored the aching stab in my heart. "My witch is the most powerful and creative magic user you'll ever meet."

"Protect them, we must," Nimbus said. "They blunder around and make dumb-dumb mistakes."

"My wonderful witch never makes mistakes," I said.

"Missing she is," Nimbus said. "Mistake that is."

"Zandra is not missing. She is... otherwise engaged."

"I'm sure Zandra will come back soon," Roland said, the pity in his eyes making my heart hurt even more. "You must miss her terribly. If I don't have Nimbus wrapped around my shoulders all the time, I miss her. Even though she's heavy and gives me a numb shoulder."

I swallowed down the lump in my throat. Roland and Nimbus had an incredible bond. It was almost as good as the one I had with Zandra.

"Mushroom beads," Nimbus said.

"What was that?" I asked.

"Check the mushroom beads, you must."

"I don't know what they are." I looked at Roland.

"Kinoko wears them around his neck," Roland said. "A long chain of beads shaped like tiny mushrooms. Why do you think they're important, Nimbus?"

"Perfect strangling tool, they would be."

"Oh! I saw his beads when we spoke, but only briefly," I said. "He tucked them inside his cloak before I could get a good look."

"Our esteemed mushroom mage didn't kill Azureus!" Roland said. "Why would he do that?"

"Shame Azureus brought to the fungi community." Nimbus hissed. "Old-fashioned smelly obsessives. Stick in the muds."

"Shame?" I asked.

Roland comforted Nimbus with a gentle hand. "I wouldn't have called it shame, but Azureus ruffled feathers by being unconventional and unapologetic about his success. We're an old-fashioned bunch and despise change. Our current mage is very... particular."

"Stick in the mud," Nimbus repeated.

Roland half-shrugged. "I got the impression he only allowed Azureus to continue his work because of his popularity. Azureus's last book was more of a fictional adventure than a reality-based factual tome. It was adored by fans but despised in the academic community. Although I believe Azureus donated a portion of the profits to our university, so the book boffins can't be too grumpy."

"It sounds like Azureus was aware he wasn't popular, so he looked for ways to secure his position," I said. "That was smart of him."

"Through bribery, he secured," Nimbus said. "Smart or sneaky?"

"No bribery. It was a very public and very generous donation," Roland said. "Azureus funded twenty full scholarships. And there was talk of him donating more money to expand the fungi research facilities. They were considering naming a new wing after him."

Nimbus grumbled to herself and shuffled on Roland's shoulders. "Silly men and their mushrooms."

"You need a nap. That'll sweeten your mood." Roland kissed the top of Nimbus's furry head.

There was a loud pop followed by a hiss and then several screams. We all turned to see a food stall had caught fire. The owner was ineffectively throwing cups of water on the flames and then dancing back and yelping as they grew higher and grabbed at the fabric roof.

"Oh, dear! Duty calls. I hope I've been helpful. And I hope you catch your man." Roland and Nimbus raced off to deal with the blaze as mushroom-doped idiots began dancing around the fire as if it were a fun adventure.

I let out a sigh of frustration. This conversation left me in a muddle and no clearer to discovering who should be my prime suspect. Gilly was open about his dislike of Azureus. Kinoko said he'd shared a mutual respect for Azureus, but if he didn't like his way of doing things, was that a lie? And was Kinoko lying because he strangled Azureus with his mushroom beads?

More laughter drifted out of the marquee Angel Force had taken over.

I twitched my whiskers. I was done muddling through this on my own. It was time to confront the angels and force them to help.

Chapter 8

Broken wings

It wasn't until I zapped Cythera in the butt with a stinging spell that I got her attention. She whirled around, her wings splayed. She held a large glass of what looked like cloudy champagne and a half-eaten sweet tart. "Oh, look, it's my least favorite feline. Come to ruin our fun, I suppose."

"You shouldn't be having fun. You should be solving Azureus's murder." I whipped my tail out of the way as two angels bounded past.

"That's your problem," Cythera said. "Either join in the party or get lost."

"You're the head of this local branch of Angel Force. That makes this murder very much your problem," I said. "Stop getting drunk and start investigating. Although I'm perfectly capable, I can't be expected to do this all on my own."

"Go bother your witch and ask for her help." Cythera smirked and nudged Bertoli, who stood beside her. "Oh, my mistake. You can't. She ditched you."

"Take that back," I snarled at Cythera. "I have a perfect partnership with Zandra."

"So where is she? Everyone knows Zandra abandoned you weeks ago. She took off partying with Vorana, and you'll never see her again."

"That's untrue. And if you were halfway decent at doing your job, you'd be looking for Zandra and Vorana. Their disappearance is unnatural."

"You're only saying that because they've abandoned you and you're looking for someone to blame. But their disappearance is on you, furball."

I drew in a breath to settle my anger. "I'm not here to discuss my missing witch. A murder was committed at this festival, and you need to look into it. The angels you left to look for the murder weapon or any clues let me down."

"That's your fault for not giving them clear instructions," Cythera said. "As stunning as my angels are physically, they're not the brightest tools in the box. You must be explicit to avoid mistakes. Over the years, I've learned that the hard way."

"Then be explicit! Do your job and make sure your angels do theirs," I said.

Cythera downed her drink and tossed the empty glass over her shoulder. "Or what? You don't control me. I've put you in charge of this case because I've got better things to do, but that doesn't mean you get to order me around."

"I've done it successfully in the past, and I'll do it again," I said. "Stop acting like an over-enthusiastic airhead at a sorority party and focus on the serious crime that's been committed in Crimson Cove."

"The serious crime that's been committed in Crimson Cove," Bertoli mocked. "Loosen up, Juno. Have a mushroom tart."

I batted away the tart he offered me, and it splatted on the ground.

"What's got your panties in a twist?" Bertoli rubbed his hand. "There was no need to use your claws."

"It got your attention," I said. "Now I have it, both of you come with me. Look at the murder scene again. Then go back to your headquarters and study the body. I've already had a look, but I don't know what tests you run on corpses."

"How did you manage to look at the body?" Cythera took a menacing step toward me. "I closed the office. My angels are all on vacation, so they can celebrate the festival. Did somebody let you in?"

"No. When I got there, the place was empty, but I found a door open."

"You mean you broke in?"

I dodged the wing Cythera swiped at me. "Maybe I did. But you left me no choice. I had to break in to check on Adrienne and Joel. They had no food and were furious."

"They're ghouls! If they get hungry enough, they'll eat each other," Cythera said. "I should charge you with breaking and entering. I expect there'll be criminal damage charges to throw in there, too."

"Juno probably stole something as well," Bertoli said. "I wouldn't be surprised if food has gone missing from the fridge. She's always sneaking into people's food stashes and taking what doesn't belong to her."

"That's right, she does. Perhaps a few hours locked in a cell with Adrienne and Joel will teach you how to behave." Cythera flared her wings wider as she swiped one at me again.

"If you lock me up, who will solve Azureus's murder?" I dodged another wing strike. This angel was relentless in her attempt to injure me. "And if this case goes unsolved, the higher angels will get involved. Do you want them poking about your business?"

"That bunch of elevated freaks can take a long walk off a short pier," Cythera said. "I get sick of their weird demands and constant rule changes that make no sense. The last committee I went to with higher angels lasted four days because one of them got lost in a different dimension. They shouldn't be allowed to use such power if they can't control it. Most of them are insane or imbeciles."

I'd never heard Cythera speak badly about the higher angels. It was a clear sign something was dreadfully wrong with her.

"Just come with me and focus on the case," I said. "If we work together, we could have this solved by the end of the day. I've already started talking to suspects."

"It's not happening. Besides, it sounds like you've gotten everything under control," Cythera said. "We're not needed. And I won't tolerate this behavior for much longer."

I hissed at her. "What behavior are you talking about?"

"The disgusting, clingy neediness you've had ever since Zandra ditched you. You're looking for her replacement, but don't waste your time staring at me or any of my angels. We all know you're unnatural and strange. Your magic reeks of burned wood and broken dreams. Who'd want to be anywhere near that?"

I flung a spell, and it whacked into Cythera's chest, causing her to stagger back. "Firstly, Zandra hasn't ditched me. And secondly, there's nothing wrong with the way my magic smells. You're just not used to being around an immensely powerful being who could kick you into another dimension if she chose to do so."

"Being?" Cythera rubbed her chest. "You make it sound like you're some elevated creature of rule rather than just another magic user."

"Juno probably thinks she's a goddess," Bertoli said. "Cats always have an over-rated opinion of themselves. I blame Egypt. The cats have never forgotten all the statues and worship."

He didn't know how close to the truth he was. Not the over-rated part, but the goddess part. "My magic isn't up for discussion. Will you help me solve this crime?"

"We'll help drink this place dry of all the mushroom-infused champagne we can get our hands on," Cythera said. "But that's it. We're on vacation. And I've given my angels triple pay while they don't work, so you won't get help from us while those rules are in place."

"Then let me give you a gift. A visual display of how twisted and messed up your heart is." I conjured another spell, leapt in the air, and twirled, covering every angel in the marquee with my magic. They shook and flapped their wings as their feathers turned a dense matt black.

While they protested and examined their new color scheme, I snagged a bunch of keys off Cythera's belt and dashed from the marquee. At least with these, I'd be able to get in and out of Angel Force easily to keep an eye on Adrienne and Joel.

I bounded away from the festival, dodging celebrating groups and crowds investigating the busy stalls. There was still a crowd dancing around the blazing food stall, but Roland had things under control. I didn't look back to see if the angels were in pursuit. If they came after me, I'd fight back. I recognized they'd been affected just like so many people in town, but I didn't have time to unpick their problems.

This murder wouldn't solve itself. And I was glad I had Azureus's death to focus upon. I'd been pining for Zandra, thinking through the possibilities of where my witch had gone. At least with a murder at the forefront of my mind, it gave me a distraction. And a welcome one. Ruminating got a cat nowhere. It was as unhelpful as a chocolate teapot and far less tasty.

I arrived back at Vorana's house, setting down the keys so I could undo the front door using my paws. It was never an easy task without opposable thumbs.

"Look out below!"

I backed to the edge of the porch and peered up at the sound of Sage's voice, just as she leapt off the top of the roof! Her front paws were splayed wide and her eyes shut.

I raced out and thrust up a spell to soften her fall. She landed with a gentle bounce and rolled several times before coming to rest on her back with a grunt.

"What did you do that for?" Sage spat at me, her ears flat against her head.

"You fell off the roof! What did you expect me to do? Watch to see if you'd bounce or splat?"

"You should have let me fall." Sage weakly swiped a paw at me. "I've made a decision. If Vorana's not here and she's not coming back, I don't want to be here either."

I stared at my grumpy friend in unmasked shock. "You deliberately jumped?"

"Of course I did."

I looked up at the roof again. "You wouldn't have died from that height. You may have broken a bone, but that would have been simple to heal."

"So says you. I could have done it. I was planning to land on my head, but then your stupid spell got in the way. Thanks for nothing."

I sighed and rolled Sage over so she lay flat on her belly, which looked much comfier. "Giving up isn't the answer."

"I don't want to live without Vorana. My world has no meaning now she's not in it."

"She is in it! Tug on your magic bond and you'll see she's right there," I said. "Go on. Do it now."

Sage huffed out a breath then closed her eyes for a second.

"What do you feel?" I asked.

"Vorana is there, but she never responds. The bond feels strained. It could break at any second."

"But it's not broken yet, and that's the most important thing," I said. "We must not give up. If we do, then I'll join you in finding the highest building in town, and we'll leap off it together, paw in paw."

"Everything is broken, and we can't fix it," Sage said. "Maybe we're broken too. That's why Zandra and Vorana abandoned us. They came to their senses and realized we're not good enough. I've got my disability, and you've got your strange old magic and secrets you hide."

"Enough of that talk. You're perfect just as you are. And my magic may be old and strange, but I keep my secrets for a reason."

"Some good it's done you," Sage said.

"Those aren't the reasons they left us," I said. "Maybe we are misshapen, and a touch broken, but isn't everybody? We all have battles to face and scars we wear, some more obviously than others. But facing challenges and coming through them makes us stronger and better. Our witches know that. That's why we're such a perfect fit for them."

Sage twitched her nose. "Some of that makes a tiny bit of sense. Fetch me my harness. I left it by the back door."

"Does that mean you'll keep helping me solve this murder?"

"Do I have a choice?"

"You can keep jumping off the roof, but I'll keep catching you," I said. "I never give up on a friend."

"You're so annoying."

"That's because I'm always right."

Fifteen minutes later, and after getting Sage up to speed with what I'd learned, she was comfortably back in her harness, and we were inside the Angel Force office again. We'd brought supplies for Adrienne and Joel, and they were munching on frozen steaks after attempting to bite us. After they'd been fed, we returned to the morgue to inspect Azureus's body again.

"He looks the same as the last time we were here." Sage remained by the door, still not wanting to get too close.

"It was something Nimbus said to me," I murmured. "Do you remember seeing a long string of beads around Kinoko's neck?"

"Sure. What do they have to do with this?" Sage asked.

"Nimbus is suspicious of Kinoko. She said he could have used those beads to strangle Azureus." My booping snooter was almost touching Azureus's cold chest as I inspected the darkening marks on his skin. "The problem is, his beads are shaped like tiny mushrooms and would have left a clear indentation, and I'm not seeing any unusual marks. Whatever was used to strangle Azureus was thin and flat. I was thinking a rope, but that would leave fibers, and I don't see anything like that on his skin."

"The mushroom mage guy was with Gilly at the time of the murder, though, wasn't he?" Sage asked.

"Maybe they're in on it together," I said. "Or maybe when Gilly was in a deep state of meditation, Kinoko snuck off and committed the murder."

"If what you told me is right, and Azureus was after Kinoko's job, it's a good motive for murder.

Kinoko could have enlisted Gilly to help him kill Azureus by offering him money or a better position in the weird old world of fungi."

"We need to look into that," I said. "Kinoko has influence in this community. Roland was practically quivering with excitement every time his name was mentioned. The role of Grand Mushroom Mage is a powerful position to command."

"With great fungi power comes great corruption," Sage said. "Never trust anyone with too much power. It makes them go strange. Just look at you."

"I'll attempt to take that as a compliment," I muttered. "I see nothing useful here. These marks couldn't have been made with a strange-shaped bead."

"So we're back to square one?" Sage asked.

A loud thudding drew my attention away from the body. "Adrienne and Joel can't be hungry already. We brought several pounds of meat from Vorana's freezer for them."

"I'll go see what they want," Sage said.

"Don't get too close. You don't want to be nipped by a grumpy ghoul."

"I know how to handle a couple of surly ghouls with bad attitudes." Sage trudged off.

I took a final look at Azureus's body and then gently covered him with a cloth. We needed to deal with this mystery fast, especially since Kinoko had his sights on Azureus's body becoming fertilizer. Maybe that was why he was so keen on claiming the body. He needed to be certain all evidence of his involvement had been destroyed.

Sage returned, a puzzled look on her face. "The ghouls aren't making that noise. Someone's banging on the main door."

"I hope it's not Cythera. Perhaps she's realized I've stolen her keys, and she wants them back."

"She's too busy getting drunk as a skunk and stuffing her face to worry about her keys," Sage said. "Should we ignore them?"

"Let's take a peek. Maybe it's a resident who needs help." We headed to the front door, and I peered through a window. A man with long dark hair and a red tattoo down one side of his face stood outside. He wore a wife beater vest and low-slung jeans. He was around sixty years old. Beside him was a small, anxious-looking elf clutching a dirty cloth.

"I don't know them," Sage said. "They must be here for the festival."

"I've seen the older guy before," I said. "But I can't place him."

The man noticed us and moved to the window. "I'm looking for an angel. You're not an angel." His words were drawn out and slurred, his voice hoarse, and his eyes were glazed.

"I'm happy to say I'm not. I'm far superior to the angels. What can we do for you?" I asked.

"Open the door."

"You're drunk," Sage said.

"Not drunk, just full of mushroom goodness. I must get in." He rattled the handle.

"I told you he was from the festival," Sage said. "Let's leave him out there. He can sleep it off.

He won't remember coming here by the time he wakes."

The nervy elf shuffled to the window. "Please, we do need to get in. This is Jim Stool. I believe you're looking after his son's body. Is Azureus in there with you?"

"Oh! This is Azureus's father?" I asked. Now I remembered where I'd seen the man. He'd been bickering with Azureus at the festival's opening night.

Jim staggered and then righted himself, wiping a hand across his vest. "Got it in one. And I'm here to collect my son's things."

Chapter 9

Meeting the family

I unlocked the main door and stepped back. "Please, come in."

"That's what I've been trying to do. You're the ones with the problem, not letting me get to my son." Jim staggered through the door, grabbing at the wall to prevent himself from falling.

"Are you unwell?" I asked.

The elf tiptoed closer. "The grief has turned him mad."

"He's not mad," Sage muttered. "Look at his eyes."

Jim was a bedraggled specimen with a stained vest, the fly of his jeans undone. His shoes were also mismatched.

"And you are?" I asked the elf. "I believe I saw you at the festival, too."

He nodded. "Reeny. Just Reeny. I belonged to Azureus, but my contract stipulates that upon his death, I'm passed to his closest relative. I must obey Jim and help him recover what he believes he's entitled to."

"I know what I'm entitled to, pipsqueak." Jim swiped a hand at Reeny. "And I can hear you gossiping about me. I've already warned you about that."

"Yes, master. Sorry, master." Reeny scurried back, his head down.

"You don't have to call him master," I said.

"I tell him what he can call me," Jim said. "Stop wasting my time and show me Azureus."

"Of course. I'm sorry for your loss," I said.

Jim waved away my words. "His things. Are they here, too?"

"Any personal possessions that were on Azureus's body are also here," I said.

Jim grunted as he followed Sage and me through the open-plan office. "Where are his van keys? Reeny said they were staying in some posh camper, but it's locked. There'll be stuff in there I'm also entitled to."

"You weren't staying together while you attended the festival?"

"As if that stuck-up jerk wanted me around any longer than necessary," Jim said. "But I'm his father, and I have rights. I get everything, don't I?"

I glanced at Sage. Jim wasn't interested in learning what had happened to his son, but only on getting his hands on his belongings.

"Please, be careful around Jim," Reeny whispered to me. "He's unstable. His mood is quick to sour, and you don't want to be around him when that happens."

"I'm sure you don't want that, either," I said.

"I bear it the best I can." Reeny tugged a grubby sleeve over a fresh bruise on his arm.

"Azureus is in here." I stopped by the morgue door. "This—"

"And his things, too?" Jim asked. "I need those."

"Everything he came in with has been set to one side," I said. "I brought Azureus in myself and checked his pockets."

"What about a bag? He usually has a bag with him. He keeps his most valuable supplies on him. That suspicious kid trusts no one. Not even me. His own father."

Azureus sounded very sensible. "There was no bag. Shall we go in?"

Jim huffed out a breath. "Let's get this over with."

I nudged the door with my head, but Jim pushed it all the way open. He strode in front of me, stopping when he saw the gurney with the cloth-covered body. "I suppose that's him?"

"It is. Would you like a few moments alone to say your goodbyes?"

"What's the point? It's not as if the kid can hear me. He didn't listen to me when he was alive, so he won't now he's dead."

"You may find it a comfort," I said.

"There's no comfort in seeing a corpse. And the dead don't talk back, so he can't tell me anything useful." Jim glanced at Azureus's body one last time. "Where are his things?"

"On the tray by the door." I failed to hide my irritation. Jim had no love for his son, only for what he could get from his death.

Jim strode over and rifled through the tray. "There's not much here. Did you take anything?"

"I'm a professional," I replied.

"That doesn't answer the question." He slid me a glance as he picked up a set of keys and turned them over. "What are you doing here, anyway? I thought the angels looked after the laws in this town."

"They're otherwise engaged," I said. "When they're busy, they hire the best freelance consultants."

"And that's you?"

"It's both of us," Sage said. "What can you tell us about your son?"

I was impressed Sage was stepping up to the plate again. After her failed attempt at jumping off the roof, I was more than a little concerned about her state of mind.

Jim shrugged. "He was my kid. He was full of his own self-importance. And now he's dead. End of story."

"Were you close?" I asked as innocently as I could.

"Azureus didn't want me in his life. He considered me an embarrassment." Jim stepped back and shook his head. "This is a damn shame."

My irritation softened. Perhaps Jim was in shock and it was just hitting him that his son was gone.

"He was no age to pass."

"Not that! Azureus's death means my easy supply is cut off," Jim said.

"Supply of what?" I asked.

"My boy knew the best spots to go fungi hunting. He could always tell which type of fungi would hit the sweet spot." Jim rubbed his hands together and licked his lips. "He was freakily smart at that kind of thing. He must have gotten that from his mother. It's not one of my talents."

"Hardly a surprise," Sage muttered to me. "I doubt this idiot has any talents, other than creating weird stains on his vest."

"From the way you're talking, it sounds as if you weren't fond of Azureus," I said to Jim.

"Why would I be? He thought he was better than me. When he got famous, he cut me out of his life."

"But you kept coming back," I said. "On the first night of the festival, I saw you two arguing. What was the argument about?"

"I'm entitled to a cut of his profits and some of his stash, but my son conveniently forgot to share. He had more money than he knew what to do with, but he was sneaky and would never tell me the best locations to get a fresh stash of fungi."

"Did you need fungi for medicinal reasons?" The glazed look in Jim's eyes suggested he used it for much more than alleviating aches and pains.

"Yeah, something like that. Azureus used to make me beg for the smallest scraps, though. He'd give me substandard product and stuff he couldn't sell, just to get me off his back."

"But it was never enough," I said. "You always wanted more."

Jim jabbed a finger at me. "I wanted my due. I raised that brat, and that was the thanks I got. He ignored me. I had to chase him down at festivals and cause a scene before he'd give me anything."

Reeny shuffled beside Jim, his narrow shoulders tensed and close to his ears.

"What did you think of Azureus?" I asked Reeny.

"Don't waste your time speaking to him," Jim said. "At least I got something out of this mess. But I expected more. And I will get it. I've been asking this little jerk where Azureus dug up the most exclusive truffles, but he keeps telling me he doesn't know."

"I promise you, master, I don't. As you know, I'm unable to lie."

"So you say," Jim said. "But Azureus must have taken you out with him. He always expected someone else to pick up his mess. He was a messy kid growing up, and he grew into an even messier adult. He never cared about anyone else. Doing what he wanted and forgetting the people who got him famous."

"You helped Azureus with his education?" I asked. "I heard he was self-taught."

"I couldn't keep the little beggar in school. I gave up on that and told him to figure things out for himself," Jim said. "School isn't all it's cracked up to be, anyway. Besides, we were always moving around, so it was a waste of time getting him enrolled and then being in another part of the country the following year."

"You and Azureus's mother home-educated him?"

"You can call it that if you like." Jim looked around. "Is this really all there is?"

"Yes. And for now, you can't take it."

Jim's head whipped around and his glassy eyes narrowed. "Why not?"

"Because your son was murdered."

Jim grunted. "I heard rumors something bad happened to him."

"We're investigating exactly what happened," I said.

"Don't bother. It makes no sense anyone would want him dead. He was a loser geek."

"A loser geek you happily exploited to get a fresh stash," Sage said.

Jim smirked. "My son. My property. My right to get something back. And didn't some moron say we do the best we can with the knowledge we have? It's not like I was given a manual on how to raise him. I put food on the table and made sure he had clean clothes and a place to sleep. What more should a father do?"

I inhaled and slowly let it out. That was barely raising a child. Ensuring they survived without being filthy and starving was the most basic level of parenthood. Where was the love in this relationship? Or the encouragement? The emotional engagement that showed a child was truly supported and wanted? From the account I was hearing, Azureus's upbringing had been miserable and bereft of kindness.

"Where is Azureus's mother?" I asked.

"Long gone. That ditzy witch didn't stick around past his thirteenth birthday. She said she couldn't handle a teenager, and it was all on me. Not that I was surprised. All the responsibilities fell on my shoulders."

"You have my deepest sympathies," I murmured.

"I don't need your sympathy. I need Azureus's things. When's the will reading?"

"That's not something we get involved in," I said. "You should speak to his legal counsel."

"They won't give me the time of day." Jim huffed out a breath and rocked back on his heels. "You'll deal with the funeral, though? I've got no money to waste on coffins and wakes. Whatever you do, keep it simple."

"I'm sure arrangements can be made," I said.

A gleam lit Jim's gaze. "If you let me access my son's funds, I'll sort something for him. Give him a proper send off."

I curled my tail around my paws and set my expression to neutral, even though my insides bubbled with anger at this greedy man's repugnant attitude. "Azureus will be appropriately cared for. Have you been at the festival this whole time?"

"Of course. I heard Azureus's name promoted as a keynote speaker and knew it would be the perfect time to connect with him. He evaded me at the last event. Sneaky little bugger slipped out the back and was gone before I could reach him. That meant I was owed double."

"Where were you on the night of Azureus's murder?" I asked.

Jim jerked back. "Why do you want to know that?"

"Because, if I've not made it clear enough, your son was murdered. We're investigating who did it and why."

"And you have an excellent motive for wanting him dead," Sage said. "You haven't even looked at your son's body, and you're already grasping around for his possessions."

Jim scowled at Sage. "You make me sound like I didn't care for him."

"You talk as if you didn't," I said. "What were you doing that night?"

"That's none of your damn business. We're leaving. I don't have to talk to you about nothing." Jim strode to the door, but Sage blocked him from getting out.

"I don't want to hurt you, old timer, but I will if you don't get out of my way." Jim kicked out at Sage.

"Tell us your alibi for the night of your son's murder, and you can leave." Sage remained steadfast, not intimidated by this bully and his booted foot. "Or don't you want his murder solved?"

"Sure I do." Jim glanced over his shoulder at me, indecision wavering in his gaze. "But this is a sham. There's no way you're official law enforcement, which means I can cause trouble for you. Put in a complaint. I know how these things work. Angel Force isn't friendly to the traveling community, but I've learned how to outsmart them. Every time they come at me, I spout legalese to mess with their heads. It gets them off my back and gives me time to move on."

"Our angels are currently distracted," I said. "So any complaint you make won't be listened to."

"Then I'll go higher. I know their ranks and who's in charge. If you don't let me leave this place right this second, I'll make life tough for both of you and have you charged with false imprisonment. You're keeping me here against my will. Reeny will back me up."

Reeny gulped. "Perhaps we should—"

"You be quiet!" Jim whacked Reeny with the back of his hand, sending him reeling. "I told you not to speak unless spoken to. Do I have to remind you about that again?"

Reeny rubbed his ear. "No, master. Sorry, master."

"Don't hit him!" I said. "House-elves are always obedient. They do everything you tell them to without punishment."

Jim bared his teeth at me. "I know how to run my own household. Keep your nose out of this, or it'll be something else we fall out over."

"My nose is very much invested in this investigation and your business," I said. "When I see an injustice done, I point it out. Touch Reeny again, and you'll be sorry."

Jim reached out a hand and flicked Reeny's ear.

Sage launched at Jim, slamming him in the chest and knocking him into the door. He pitched over as it opened behind him, and he slammed to the floor. Sage moved like greased lightning, her harness smacking repeatedly into Jim's face as she whirled in a dazzling spark of magic and rage.

I gently encouraged Reeny out of the way as Sage unleashed her fury on Jim. "Don't get involved. Sage has anger issues she's working through, so it's better she does that on Jim than on you."

Reeny hesitated, his body trembling as he stared at Sage. "I... I should help my master."

"Why would you do that?"

"To protect him."

"Think about all the times he's whacked you or yelled at you since you joined his household. I imagine that'll take some time. When you're done, Sage will be finished, so you can go about your day with a clear conscience."

"I'll... yes! I'll look away. If I can't see what's going on, then I can't offer help." Reeny turned his back and closed his eyes, whispering to himself, his hands clasped in front of him.

I sauntered over to a prostrate Jim. Sage sat on his face, her butt nestled against his nostrils. "Are you prepared to tell us your alibi now?"

Jim muffled something against Sage's butt and then gagged.

"Shuffle over an inch," I said to Sage. "Let the man breathe."

"The idiot doesn't deserve to breathe." Sage moved over anyway.

"I never liked cats. You're disgusting," Jim said. "Always sitting your butts where they shouldn't be. On tables where people eat. On the couch where I sit. Nasty."

"If you intend to insult us, I'll ask Sage to move back to her original position," I said. "Give us your alibi for the night of your son's murder, and this embarrassment will all be over."

Jim turned his head away and growled out his annoyance. "I was on a date. I picked up some easy-looking piece of skirt at the festival and took her to a local café in town. Some place that welcomes vampires, so we didn't hang around for long. Those cold-bloods give me the creeps."

"We know the place. It's an excellent café," I said. "What was the lady's name?"

He smirked. "She was no lady. That's why I chose her."

"Her name. And a description." I lifted a murder mitten and flared my claws.

"Calm down! I only got a first name. Florence. She was short, skinny, with blonde hair. Had all these feathers tied to the ends of her hair. You won't find her, though. There are too many people at the festival. She's probably hooked up with someone else by now and is passed out in their tent. That girl loved to party hard."

"You'll be surprised what truths I can uncover when I set my mind to it," I said. "If you behave, Sage will let you up."

Jim squirmed under Sage's weight. "I didn't come here for no trouble. But I will get what I'm due."

"I'm sure you will, once you've gone through the proper channels," I said. "Will you behave?"

Jim wrinkled his nose at Sage's looming butt. "I wish I'd never wasted my time coming here."

"I'm sure Azureus felt the same." Sage leaped off Jim's chest, making sure to whack him on the side of the head one more time with her harness.

Jim rolled to his feet and glowered at Sage. "I'll be reporting you."

Sage hissed at him, and Jim quickly backed away.

"Careful, my friend," I cautioned. "Jim won't be a bother to anyone else while he's in Crimson Cove, will you?"

Jim's fingers flexed, but he made the wise choice and didn't come after us. "I wouldn't kill my son. He was a geek and a saddo, which means he was zero threat to me."

"We've gotten all the information we need from you, so you need to leave," I said. "And I suggest you don't come back."

"Let's get out of here." Jim gestured for Reeny to follow him as he walked back along the corridor, muttering to himself.

Reeny shot over to me, a vision of tense nerves and shivers. "Meet me tomorrow at dawn. We're staying in a red campervan on the edge of your woods. I have something important to tell you."

"Come on! Don't make me hit you again," Jim yelled.

Reeny flinched and scurried away.

Sage settled beside me, washing her face with a paw. "What do you make of that jerk?"

"I think we may have just found our killer," I said.

Chapter 10

Elf secrets and lies

The next day, it was an early start. I was intrigued by what Reeny had whispered to me before dashing after Jim yesterday. I could only imagine his information had something to do with Jim's alibi. And since Jim was winning the trophy for the World's Worst Father this year, I wouldn't put it past him to commit murder to get his grasping hands on his son's fortune. But before we could prove his guilt, we had Jim's alibi to check and Reeny's information to gather.

After a quick inspection of my glorious fur to make sure it was its usual perfection, I headed up the main staircase in Vorana's house to wake Sage. She was still sleeping in Vorana's bedroom, but not on the bed—right inside the door, so she would feel any vibrations if Vorana came up the stairs.

Her eyes were closed, but one ear flicked as I stared at her. "Today is not the day to have a lie-in. We have a case to solve."

"I'm sick," Sage muttered.

"You're sad. There's a difference."

"Sadness leads to physical sickness. I read that in one of Vorana's books." Sage huffed a breath through her nose. "It said a person can make themselves unwell by having a negative mindset and not finding an outlet for their anger or sadness."

"Is that what's happened here? Overnight, you developed a serious ailment because of your misery?"

"Yes. And you most likely have it, too."

"What's this illness called?"

"Abandonitis with a rare strain of misery flu. There's no cure. And it's contagious, so if you don't already have it, stay far away from me. And no more unwanted rescues, either. If I want to jump, let me."

"This dying in despair situation must stop." I smoothed some of Sage's ruffled, crusty fur back into place. "I need my companion by my side to help solve this murder. I can't do it alone."

"You wouldn't want me around if Zandra was here," Sage said.

I huffed softly. It was true. I desired Zandra's company over everybody else's. "We know how special and unique our bond is with our witches. Nothing surpasses that. I'm not attempting to replace Zandra with you, but the world feels better when you have someone beside you, looking out for you, and helping you. We can do that for each other."

Sage grunted and possibly farted. "You behave like you don't even miss Zandra."

I dabbed my curmudgeonly friend hard on the head with a paw. "That's untrue. Every time my heart beats, I think about her. I wonder what she's doing and if she's in trouble. I hope Zandra is safe. I long for her to come back, and she will when she's ready. Everything about Crimson Cove has been turned upside down, and that includes the bonds with our witches."

Sage opened one eye. "Why are we wasting our time on this murder? We should look into what's causing the strangeness in town."

"Perhaps they're related," I said. "The most recent murders have all been tainted with oddness. The cases were solved, but never to my complete satisfaction."

"Odd how?"

"When I've been unable to sleep, I've been going over the crimes." I settled in beside Sage. She'd definitely broken wind, but I wouldn't complain about it. "We had Remus's vampire friend, Altruist, staked by his long-time girlfriend because she thought he was a terrifying monster hellbent on destroying her."

"Wasn't she under the influence of those weird herbs that got mixed up in the pizza parlor?"

"That's right. It was fortunate for her that Altruist had safely stored his original heart so he could regenerate. Otherwise, she'd have gone down for his murder. Then we have Nahla and Petra's murders."

"They were explained. The crazy husband did it. What was his name?"

"Ivan. He'd been drugged for years to remain obedient to a wife he no longer wanted to be with," I said. "I understood Ivan's motive for wanting to destroy Nahla. But he was also charged with murdering Petra."

"He confessed to that, didn't he?"

"Yes, but the methods of murder were so different. And Ivan seemed uncertain about what he'd done to Petra."

"The man's brain was addled by so many powerful herbs and spells that he didn't know what he was saying or doing most of the time," Sage said.

"And now we have Azureus's murder," I said. "In the middle of a festival that celebrates all things magical fungi. There are fifty stalls in town selling products that are powerful and have mind-altering properties. And the victim was in the heart of that world."

"Are you saying these murders are all connected?" Sage actually lifted her head, finally interested.

"You've said it yourself. The strange happenings in Crimson Cove began around the time Remus's antagonistic friend was staked on a tree. Since then, residents have grown stranger, and the town's atmosphere has felt out of control. Angel Force has been run off its feet tackling misbehaving magic users, and animal control is inundated with calls about dangerous creatures roaming around and causing mischief."

Sage grunted. "At least you don't need to worry about work."

I nodded. Barney had closed animal control without warning. Even though Zandra was gone, I'd been going into work to help where I could, but I'd arrived one morning to find a note left on the door that said: *Gone fishing. Won't be back soon.*

"In a way, I'm glad animal control is shut. It's one less thing to think about. But it's so out of character for Barney."

"Not at the moment, since everyone is being weird," Sage said.

"True. People are behaving the opposites of themselves. When they're normally caring, they're now cold and cruel. Where they'd once been funny, they're dour and miserable."

"You've got that look on your face," Sage said.

"The one that makes me particularly attractive in natural daylight?"

"The one that tells me you're putting puzzle pieces together."

"I'm attempting to, but I haven't gotten them in the right order yet," I said. "Let's go to the kitchen and forage for breakfast. Then we're visiting Reeny to find out what secrets he's keeping."

After more cajoling, I convinced Sage to head downstairs. Despite her protests that she wasn't hungry, she ate a whole bowl of kibble. We were down to the last few days of kibble rations. We'd have to start eating less palatable food soon unless I raided the freezer to defrost tuna steaks.

We were out the door just as the sun was lifting and walked the silent streets toward the edge of Crimson Cove woods. There was a large campsite tucked out of the way that was used during holiday season. It was packed with tents and a range of different-sized campervans as people stayed to enjoy the long weekend of mushroom festival fun.

"We're looking for a red campervan," I muttered as we perused the temporary homes.

"Reeny won't be any use to us," Sage said. "He's got to stay loyal to his master."

"Reeny despises his new master," I said. "But we'll need to be inventive in how we ask the questions, so we get the truth out of him. Over there. That beat-up looking campervan. That's Jim's style."

"Tasteless, smelly, and past its best?"

I smirked at Sage's accurate description. As we were approaching the campervan, there was a crash from inside and a yell, followed by a high-pitched squeak. The door slammed open, and Jim stomped out, shirtless, with only one shoe on. He strode away into the woods, clutching an off-white vest.

A few seconds later, Reeny poked his head out of the van. He looked like he'd just had a bucket of water thrown over him, his clothes sticking to his thin body. He saw us and waved us over. "I caused a distraction to get Jim out of the way, so we could talk without being disturbed."

"Did he hit you again?" I asked.

"I've had worse. Hurry! We may not have long. Jim is washing off in the stream." Reeny ushered us into the campervan, closing the door behind us. "I watched from the window, so I knew when to encourage him out."

"What did you do?" I glanced around the shabby, faded interior.

"Poured last night's cooking water over his head. I stumbled and lost my balance. At least, that's what Jim assumed happened."

"Is it true you can't lie?" Sage asked.

Reeny nodded. "I'm a particular breed of elf who has an inability to tell untruths."

"What about revealing secrets about those you're enslaved to?" I asked. "For example, can you tell us if you saw Jim strangle Azureus?"

Reeny clutched a dishcloth in his hands, wiping it ineffectively over his sodden clothing. "There are ways around every bond. But if Jim tells me not to talk about a particular topic, it causes me physical pain if I attempt to."

"How did you come to be owned by this family?" I asked.

"To clear a debt," Reeny said. "My uncle raised me, but he was an unreliable elf. He tried to game the system, but he always lost. He found himself in terrible debt with no easy way out, so he sold me into slavery. Azureus bought me, and as part of the contract, I remain with his family even after his death."

"You're unhappy about that." It wasn't a question.

Reeny winced. "There are many things in this world that would bring me much more joy. I hope Jim is the killer, so I don't have to work for him anymore."

"Won't you be passed on to someone else in the family?" Sage asked.

"Fortunately for me, Azureus has no more family," Reeny said. "Well, he has a mother, if she's still alive, but she abandoned him a long time ago. If Jim is charged with murder, the contract becomes void. I'll be free. I can finally live my own life."

"While I appreciate your honesty," I said, "that information gives you a solid motive to kill members of the Stool family."

Reeny squeaked, and his face paled. "Not me! I didn't do it."

"It's a solid motive," Sage said. "Sold into slavery by your family, working for Azureus, and then passed on to his messed-up father."

"And you said you've had worse treatment. Did Azureus also mistreat you?" I asked.

Reeny hung his head. "He did his best. He could be kind. I knew what would happen to me if Azureus died. I wanted out of my contract, but murder wasn't the way to go about it. As you can see, my new position is much worse."

"Couldn't you have bought your way out of the contract?" I asked.

"Although Azureus was wealthy, he wasn't generous to me. You often find that with people who have lots of money. They cling to their wealth for fear of losing it. Those who are the most generous have the least, and those who have the most give the least, even though they can afford it."

"That's how the rich stay rich," Sage said.

Reeny let out a sad little huff. "I can honestly say with no restrictions on my truth-telling, Azureus paid me a pittance. He had it written into the contract. My uncle received a lump sum, which paid off his debts, but I only received a token weekly payment. And Azureus took most of that as rent. Although I was never sure what I was renting. When I traveled with him, I was lucky if I got a shed to sleep in."

"You didn't like Azureus?" I asked Reeny.

Reeny closed his eyes for several seconds and breathed in deeply. "Azureus was very smart and garnered respect from many. His work brought him great pride, so I was proud as well."

"That's your roundabout way of saying you didn't like him?" Sage asked.

"I... never say a bad word about anyone."

"You just said you hoped Jim was a murderer," I said.

Reeny blushed. "Almost never. I'm never cruel with my words. If I can't be nice, then I'm quiet."

"You must have hated working for someone who paid you so poorly and didn't treat you well," I said. "You can nod if it makes things easier."

Reeny pressed his lips together and nodded.

"And you've gotten an even worse bargain by being passed on to Jim," I said.

"I can't disagree with that," Reeny said. "You should look at him as the killer. That's why I brought you here. I have to show you something. Follow me."

We headed into a small, ripe-smelling bedroom, the bedding long past the acceptable date for being washed. Numerous items of clothing and food containers had been tossed on the floor.

"Doesn't Jim order you to clean for him?" I picked my way around the food cartons.

"He doesn't think it's important," Reeny said. "Or more likely, it's not crossed his mind. He's usually so..."

"Away with the mushroom fairies?" Sage asked. "He's got a problem, hasn't he?"

"That's a polite way of putting it." Reeny flipped open the lid of an old tin box, revealing several dozen packages and wraps of different types of dried mushrooms. "This is his own stash." He opened a bigger box, revealing even more varieties of dried mushrooms, toadstools, and truffles. "And this is what he deals."

"Does Jim have a license to sell all of this?" I asked.

"Of course not. But that's why he always hounded Azureus. Azureus had access to different types of fungi, and to get his father off his back, he'd give him some. Azureus would tell Jim it was only for personal use and he must never sell it or give it to anybody else. Jim never listened. He takes the fungi and cuts it with rubbish, then sells it as a premium product." Reeny groaned and doubled over, clutching his stomach.

"Jim told you not to tell anybody that, didn't he?" I placed a paw on Reeny's forehead and covered him in healing magic to alleviate his pain.

"He's a monster. All he wants is money and fungi. He cares about nothing else. I can't live like this. I need to be free. And if that means hurting myself to get the truth out there so that evil creature is put behind bars, then I'll do it."

"Was Jim telling the truth about his alibi?" I asked.

"I couldn't tell you where he was that night. I was still obligated to Azureus."

"Did you see where Azureus went just before he died?" I asked. "Why did he go behind that marquee?"

"I don't know. He sent me away. He liked to be alone after a busy event. Azureus would often go walking and sometimes wore a disguise, so he wouldn't be recognized. He enjoyed the fame, but he grew weary of the adulation. I didn't see what happened to him or who did it."

"I expect he wishes he wore a false beard and wig on the night he was killed," Sage said. "It could have saved him."

"What did you do after Azureus sent you away?" I asked.

"I was exhausted. I went to sleep," Reeny said.

"Where do you sleep?"

"Under whatever vehicle my master uses," Reeny said. "Azureus owned a deluxe camper on the edge of the site. He parked away from everybody else. I was under there."

"I'm assuming you were under there alone," I said.

"Of course. I'd be embarrassed to take anybody under there with me. What a dreadful thought."

I stared at the dried mushroom stash. Reeny had a strong alibi and no motive for the time of Azureus's death. And he was pointing hard at Jim as the killer. Was that the truth or was he deflecting?

There was a crash outside, followed by gruff cussing.

Reeny jumped into action. "That must be Jim. He'll be furious if he catches you here. Out! You have to go."

We were bundled out of the campervan just as Jim appeared, wringing out his vest. We ducked out of sight around the side of the van and waited until he'd gone inside and slammed the door before speaking.

Sage yawned. "Would you call that progress?"

"Of sorts. Jim is an unstable, addicted dealer with rage issues, but Reeny must be a suspect, too. Sold into slavery and working for a family that doesn't respect him."

"And he has a lousy alibi," Sage said. "No alibi, in fact."

"Very true. This mystery grows ever more complicated."

"What now?"

"We fix some ghoul friendly breakfast and plan our next move to catch a killer."

Chapter 11

Pink surprise

We returned to Angel Force, a place that felt like my second home since we were visiting so frequently. Once again, we'd raided Vorana's fridge and brought in some out-of-date, defrosted corned beef. It didn't matter if it was a little on the ripe side since ghouls weren't fussy about what they ate, so long as it was protein packed.

"Watch your paws!" I gently nudged Sage out of the reach of Adrienne and Joel's snapping teeth.

"They can't get through the magic," Sage said.

"They want to, though. One missed paw step from us, and it'll be the end."

Sage narrowed her eyes and peered at the ghouls.

I batted her several times on the head with a paw. "Don't even think about it. That's no way to go out. Vorana would be heartbroken to find you turned into a ghoul."

"How would she know, since she's never coming back?"

"She is. No more morbid thoughts. We have a murder board to set up." I returned to the empty open-plan office and walked to the clean whiteboard used to set out the evidence in a new case. That was when I realized the problem. How were we supposed to write on the whiteboard?

I knocked a board marker down and pulled off the cap with my teeth. I didn't want to use it and stain my fur. I'd yet to fully recover from my unplanned dunking in a cauldron of melting corpse and magical tea.

"I've got a spell to help with that." Sage trundled over. "You say what you want on the board, and I'll magic it on."

"Excellent. You see how valuable you are? If you turned into a ghoul, you wouldn't be able to write on anything. You'd be too busy chewing on the poor person you'd hunted and savaged."

"I'm just thinking through the options," Sage said. "I've lived a good life, but I'm long in the tooth, not that I have many teeth left, so I need to decide what happens next."

"Your bond with Vorana sustains you," I said. "It's one of the many benefits of bonding with a powerful magic user. You live at least as long as them."

"But with her gone, it all seems pointless," Sage said. "I didn't mind the occasional aching joint and stiff muscle when I was with Vorana. I was happy to put up with it, but not now."

"Once this is over, we'll find the perfect healing spell for you. That'll get rid of the aches and pains. You don't have to suffer. There's no point in being a martyr when you don't have to be. I assure you, it impresses no one and irritates many," I said.

"Less judging me and more focusing on this murder." Sage sparked a spell between her paws. "Who's first?"

"Jim Stool, Azureus's father, needs to be up the top. We must check his alibi or see if we can find anyone who'll place him close to the marquee where Azureus died. He's got a lot to gain from his son's death."

Sage flung out the spell, and spidery black words filled the whiteboard.

"We need Reeny on there, too," I said. "I'm still not sure if I believe him when he says he can't lie. And was he deflecting onto Jim? He was most insistent we focus on him."

"I can see why," Sage said. "Get Jim out of the picture, and he's a free elf."

"Reeny has a strong motive too, and no alibi. Sleeping alone under a campervan isn't good enough for me."

Sage flung the information onto the murder board. "Reeny seems a bit weedy to be a killer. Submissive. I can't imagine him even raising his voice, let alone strangling someone."

"He's most likely docile from his enforced years of servitude," I said. "He never wanted to serve this family, and he must feel bitter toward his uncle for selling him so he could clear his debts. It was a selfish and inconsiderate move to inflict on such a young elf."

Sage put more information on the board. "Who's next?"

"Gilly Piper," I said.

"We should put him and Kinoko, the mushroom mage, next to each other," Sage said. "They're each other's alibi."

"Agreed. They tie in where they land on the suspect list," I said. "Gilly wasn't complimentary about Azureus, and I suspect there's a degree of jealousy over Azureus's fame and popularity."

"And we've also been hearing that Kinoko thought little of Azureus, too," Sage said.

"Azureus's non-traditional way of gaining entry into the fungi community has gone down badly in many circles," I said. "Since Gilly and Kinoko are each other's alibis, they're either telling the truth and are both innocent, or they're lying and they did it together." I nodded as the information settled on the board. "We should ask around at the festival, see if anyone noticed them wandering about when they should have been meditating. And even if they were meditating, we saw with Altruist's almost murder what happens when someone ingests the wrong fungi."

"They get staked on a tree by their own sharp-toothed honey bun," Sage said.

"Exactly. Did they get high on the wrong substance and strangle Azureus, thinking he was dangerous?"

Sage moved back to fully examine the board. "That's it, isn't it?"

"I want Roland Moldsworth on there, too," I said.

"Roland's no killer. He'd die of fright if he tried anything so risky," Sage said. "Besides, didn't he say he was with Nimbus?"

"Yes, but a familiar will always side with their bonded magic user, so Nimbus could be lying to protect Roland."

"Why would Roland kill Azureus?"

"I don't think he did, not really, but he discovered the body. Perhaps Roland committed the crime, and we almost caught him in the act. He faked fainting to make sure he appeared innocent." Given what I knew about Roland, it was the unlikeliest of scenarios, but we couldn't dismiss him.

"I'll eat my harness if it was Roland, but he can go on there if he has to." Sage thrust out a spell, and Roland's name appeared on the board. "Is that it?"

"Now we make a plan. We can start by checking Jim's alibi to see if he was on a date. That'll be easy to do by visiting Sorcha's café."

"And eat lunch while we're there." Sage nodded. "We can also go to the festival and ask around to see if anyone saw Roland acting shady. Also Kinoko and Gilly."

"And we need to find out what fungi they used before entering their meditation," I said. "If they used the wrong substance, they could have hallucinated the worst and acted on it."

"What about Reeny?" Sage asked.

"We need to find a way to see if he'll lie," I said. "If he's unable to tell untruths, then he's already revealed his innocence, since he said he didn't kill Azureus."

There was a crash in the reception area, and a few seconds later, a teary-eyed blonde in a form-fitting pink dress appeared in the doorway. "He's dead! My angel is dead."

I hurried over to the woman. "Did you say an angel was dead?" She was classically pretty, with a button nose, full lips, and big blue eyes.

"No, not an angel. My angel. My honey pie. Is Azureus here?"

"Oh! You were Azureus's girlfriend?" I asked.

She pulled a large white handkerchief from a tiny pink glittering purse and loudly blew her nose. "We didn't like labels. They're too confining. But we were involved."

Sage walked over and joined us. "He's here. What's your name?"

"Selena Sparkle. Are you in charge?"

"We're jointly managing this investigation," I said, making the introductions.

Selena blinked several times, her eyes sparkling with tears. "Where are all the angels? Shouldn't they be doing something about this terrible death? My honey boo is gone. Why isn't everyone crying?"

"There's a festival in town that has caught the angels' attention." I gestured to some seats.

Selena tottered over in a pair of pink heels encrusted with rhinestones and sank into one. "I only heard about Azureus's death this morning. Why didn't anyone get in touch with me sooner? I'm his significant other."

"I'm sorry for your loss," I said. "Things have been tricky in town."

"And we didn't know Azureus had a non-labeled girlfriend," Sage said.

Selena dabbed at her plump cheeks with the tissue, carefully blotting so as not to disturb her perfect makeup. "Azureus insisted on coming to these dreadful things. I never wanted to attend. He always refused to pay for a hotel, so we had to stay in his grubby camper. I did it once and swore never again. But then I missed him, so I came for a surprise visit. When I got to the festival, I heard people gossiping about someone dying. I was stunned when I learned it was Azureus."

"We're all surprised about what happened," I said.

"I sent him so many messages, and he didn't reply to a single one."

"Being dead would make that tricky," Sage said.

Selena sniffed up tears. "I have a ton of luggage, but I couldn't manage it on my own. I was hoping he'd pick me up and settle me into the hotel I've booked."

"Where are you staying?" I asked.

"The Sleepy Stardust Sanctuary," Selena said. "It was the best I could find. It is the best in town, isn't it?"

"The finest. I'm sure something can be sorted with your luggage. The owner, Lizzie Briar, is very capable," I said.

"I don't believe that. I couldn't find anyone working at the hotel. I had to grab my own key from behind the desk! The whole thing was a shambles. Azureus always looked after me." Selena hiccupped. "He was good like that. What happened to him?"

"We can't reveal too much," I said. "But his death wasn't from natural causes."

Selena's mouth turned down. "I heard all the gross murder whispers. Have you caught the person who did it?"

"Not yet. We're still gathering information. It's early days."

"Where did he die?"

"At the festival."

"I always told him these festivals were bad news." Selena's gaze hardened a fraction as she studied me and then Sage. "What qualifications do you have to solve this crime?"

"We're the best in town," I said.

"In truth, we're the only ones in Crimson Cove with any interest in this mystery," Sage said. "Angel Force has gone on an extended vacation, and they're off stuffing their faces and getting stoned at the mushroom festival."

I chastised my friend with a stern look, even though she spoke the truth.

Selena jumped as Adrienne and Joel slammed around and kicked their door. "What have you got back there?"

"Troublemakers, but they're secured, so you're safe," I said. "You've arrived in Crimson Cove during a difficult time. Perhaps you should return home."

"I'm staying until you figure out what happened to my Azureus," Selena said. "Poor sweetie pie angel. I shall miss him. He was always so generous with his gifts, if not the hotel rooms. He'd buy me a gift at least once a week, when I whined long enough. He was such a tease."

Would Selena miss Azureus or only his gifts? "As you wish. Do you have anyone with you?"

"No, I spent most of my free time with Azureus and a few other close friends." Selena pulled out a small compact mirror and tidied her makeup. "Since I'm here, I'll take his personal effects."

"That won't be possible," I said.

She placed her mirror back in her purse and stared at me. "Why not? I know he left me everything."

"Azureus left you his estate?" I didn't know how wealthy he'd been, but since Selena wasn't the only one after his assets, Azureus must have had a sizeable fortune.

"Of course! Azureus said he wrote me into his will, so I'm entitled to it all. We were practically married."

"In a non-labeled, non-exclusive way?" Sage muttered.

I glanced at Sage. This was interesting information. Selena was now a new suspect with a brand-new motive. Get put into her boyfriend's will and then bump him off.

"Azureus always carried plenty of money. I can at least have that, can't I?" Selena pouted. "I'll need to pay for my hotel room."

"We can't return any items that belonged to Azureus until the investigation is closed," I said. "And Azureus's father, Jim, is here. He also has an interest in Azureus's belongings."

Selena's eyes widened a fraction. "Huh! I didn't think he'd show his face."

"You seem surprised," I said.

"I... I am! They weren't close. Jim used to pester Azureus when he wanted a fresh supply of fungi. The man's brain is addled by using too much of the stuff. He has no self-control. I was always telling Azureus to be careful around him."

"There were problems between Azureus and his father?" I asked.

"Jim only ever got in touch with Azureus when he wanted something. He'd play the interested father role for five minutes then turn the conversation to himself and his needs. Such a selfish man." Selena lifted a finger. "And don't believe a word he tells you. Jim is only here for what he can get out of Azureus. A free place to stay. Money. Fungi. Even a free ride somewhere. He's always take, take, take."

"That's good to know," I said.

"But I was Azureus's main companion, and I'm sure I'm a beneficiary in his will, so I need my fair cut, too." Selena fluttered her lashes. "We've been dating on and off for years, and Azureus adored me. He wanted to make an honest woman of me, but I'm too free-spirited for ceremonies and rings."

"Or being faithful," Sage whispered to me.

"Do you live nearby?" I asked Selena.

"No, I'm a nomad. I follow Azureus around for some of the year, but then I vacation somewhere hot and tropical. I must keep my tan topped up. The boys love a tan." She flashed us a long, bronzed leg.

"You have no place of your own?" Sage asked.

"If I ever found myself lacking accommodation, Azureus put me up in the best hotels. He was a generous sweetie when I needed him to be."

From what I was learning about Selena, she was a manipulative gold digger. The second she left, she was going on the murder board.

"Is there anything I can say or do to convince you to let me have Azureus's things?" Selena asked. "Even the keys to his camper will do. I can take a peek inside and make sure he didn't leave anything special lying around. We wouldn't want it to get into the wrong hands now, would we?"

"We definitely wouldn't, and I wish we could be more helpful," I said. "But if we start giving his things away, we could miss a vital clue that helps us figure out who killed Azureus. We wouldn't want that now, would we?"

Selena pouted again, and there was more eyelash fluttering. "Are you sure? Could I give you a belly rub? Brush your fur? I'll be gentle. Make you purr."

"We're not dogs, rolling over like goofy idiots for a stomach rub. And never touch a cat's belly unless you have a clear invitation," I said. "Even then, I'd advise caution."

The pout vanished, and Selena glanced at the wall clock. She jumped up. "I must go! The Grand Mushroom Mage is about to demonstrate his new three-times-filtered truffle dust. It's billed as an out-of-this-world experience. Toodles." She dashed away as quickly as she'd arrived.

"That was an experience I don't want to repeat anytime soon," Sage said. "Selena doesn't care about Azureus being dead. She's just like Jim and wants to get those fake nails into Azureus's fortune."

"And because of that, Selena has planted herself in the middle of the suspects," I said. "This mystery has gotten even more complicated."

"Does that mean we can step back and let someone qualified take over?"

I gently head-butted my surly friend. "It means we must be extra focused to ensure we catch our killer."

Chapter 12

Luncheon meat

"We should at least try before we visit Sorcha. That mouse is so close I can almost taste it," I said, catching the distinctive whiff of a hot, furry body within leaping distance.

"The last thing I successfully hunted was an already dead, partially rotting bat carcass left in Vorana's backyard," Sage said. "There's no way this will work. Let's stay focused on the crime. Isn't that what you keep moaning on about?"

"I never moan. You must make an effort. You never know what you can achieve when you put your mind to it."

"If you tell me practise makes perfect, I'm bopping you on the end of your nose," Sage said.

"We'll catch nothing if you keep talking so loudly," I whispered. "Follow me. And the exercise will do you good. You've been loafing about on that prickly mat in the kitchen for far too long. You've lost muscle tone."

"My muscles are in peak condition," Sage said. "It's everything else that's messed up. How am I supposed to chew on a mouse with these teeth? Let's go to the café. Sorcha will warm up bone broth for me. I can slurp that down with no trouble."

"If we catch the mouse, we'll gift it to Sorcha. She loves that sort of thing."

"I've yet to meet anything on two legs that enjoys prey gifts." Sage slumped beside me as I sniffed the air and determined where our target was.

My gaze narrowed. "Twenty paw steps north."

"Your paw steps or mine? I sometimes hobble and shuffle, so it'll take me longer."

"Mine."

"And which way is north?"

"Head toward the big tree with the broken bough."

We shuffled closer on our bellies, Sage's harness squeaking as we approached.

"It's time you got that thing oiled," I muttered.

"I'll take it to the garage the next time I have a spare minute, shall I?"

"Less grousing, more sniffing."

Sage muttered something rude about me under her breath as she continued skulking. I was almost within reach of the mouse when I realized Sage was no longer with me. I turned to see her about to bite into a random fungus that sprouted out of the base of a tree.

I raced back and batted her nose away before she could bite down. "You don't know if it's safe to consume! And since when did you get interested in eating vegetables?"

"I'm hoping it's poisonous. I give up! I've tried to be cheerful and optimistic, and it made me feel worse. There's nothing to all that nonsense about telling yourself positive affirmations to make you happier. It's doing the opposite to me. I feel lousy and hopeless. And a dumb fraud."

"Because you're focused on the wrong thing." I deliberately sat on the mushroom so Sage couldn't eat it. "It would be easy to give up, lay on the prickly mat, and make no decision, but don't you realize what you're doing when you do that?"

"Finding peace?" Sage asked. "No longer being bothered by you?"

"By not deciding, you're making a decision to freeze in place and not take positive action. That's a hindrance for anybody. That's a stagnant life choice."

"Maybe I like stagnant. And I don't want to be a hindrance to you. Leave me here with the mushrooms. I'll sort myself out."

I gently pushed Sage away from the possibly poisonous fungus. "What I mean is you think you're not doing anything by saying you give up, but you're making a huge decision, and it's the wrong one. Inaction of any kind is still a choice. You're choosing not to fight."

Sage hissed at me. "I have been fighting. You know how many spells I've cast to find Vorana and how many hours I've walked around the town calling for her."

"And when she gets back, she'll be delighted by how diligent you've been."

"She won't be delighted when she sees the mess we've made of her pantry," Sage said.

"Vorana will understand. We're doing what we need to do to stay alive. It's a good thing."

"Hunting mice isn't a good thing," Sage said. "I don't even like their taste. I only catch them to give them to Vorana."

I glanced over my shoulder, but the distinctive smell of the mouse was long gone. "To be honest, so do I. For Zandra, not Vorana. I'm not a fan of rodent. I want to find the perfect mouse to give to Zandra to make her happy. Her reactions so far have ranged from disgust to ear-splitting screaming. There must be a rodent gift she likes. I even tried a frog's leg. Not a success."

"If they ever come back, we can keep hunting until we find the answer," Sage said.

"That's more like it. Keep your hopes up. We'll indulge in a huge lunch, get answers from Sorcha, and feel better."

Sage stared longingly at the mushroom then followed me out of the woods and into the main part of town toward Sorcha's café. I was relieved to see the door open. Her hours had been as irregular as a constipated bear with an irritable bowel. And when I'd been in to ask how Sorcha was doing and if she had news about Zandra or Vorana, she'd been offhand to the point of curtness.

There were a few people in the café, mainly buying carry out food, which I assumed they'd be taking to the mushroom festival. We entered and headed to the counter. Before I had a chance to speak to Sorcha, Denver, her boyfriend, rushed past us with a huge bouquet of red roses. I barely recognized him, as he wore wraparound sunglasses, a thick black cloak, and a black baseball cap pulled down low. The sun was rarely kind to younger vampires.

"Please give me another chance." He thrust the roses at Sorcha. "Whatever I've done, I'll make it right. Just say you forgive me and take me back."

Sorcha didn't look up from the bread she buttered. "You're wasting your time and your money on those flowers. Not interested."

"Tell me what the problem is and I'll fix it," Denver said. "I'll do anything. We were getting along so well, and then you dropped me like a hot stone. What did I do that was so wrong?"

Sorcha stabbed the knife into the bread and finally looked at him. When she did, the only emotion shining in her eyes was disapproval. "We don't work. You're basically dead. It's creepy."

Denver spluttered several words that made no sense. "But you're mostly vampire. You've always welcomed vampires into your café, and I thought you'd welcomed me into your heart."

"Having you around makes me uncomfortable. I don't want you here. We're wrong for each other. If you don't leave, I'll call Angel Force."

"Good luck with that," I muttered.

"Did you know there was trouble in paradise?" Sage asked me.

"Not a clue. The last I heard, they were getting along famously. But Sorcha's been affected just like everybody else in town, so it's no wonder she's acting out of character."

Sorcha snatched the flowers and whacked Denver with them. "And you can take these roses and shove them up your—"

"Greetings, Sorcha! We'll order two smoked salmon plates," I said.

Sorcha stopped insulting Denver and glanced over the counter top. "I was about to close."

"And miss the lunchtime rush?" I said. "I'm happy to see business is booming again."

"What do I care?" Sorcha threw the roses at Denver. "I'm about to receive an offer on this place."

"Are you leaving too?" I gently nudged Denver's ankle as I walked past him. He was crestfallen, the damaged bouquet hanging limply by his side.

"I thought I'd join Zandra and Vorana. Let my hair down and have some fun."

I hopped onto the counter, my heart skipping several beats. "You've heard from Zandra?"

Sorcha scowled at me. "Off! No fur in the food. It's unhygienic."

"But you've heard from Zandra?"

"Or Vorana?" Sage asked.

"No, but I'll head out and see where fate takes me. And they can't be that difficult to find," Sorcha said. "So long as they want to be discovered."

"We'll come with you," Sage said.

"No baggage," Sorcha said. "But I'm glad you've come in, Juno. I want you to look after the kittens while I'm gone. They're a pain in the behind, but you should be able to manage them."

"You've not found them a home yet?" A few weeks ago, Sorcha fostered three adorable, immensely powerful, feral black kittens. I'd made friends with them, but had almost forgotten about them, given everything else that was going on.

"No one is interested in them," Sorcha said. "I can't say I'm surprised. They set fire to things and cause chaos. I'll be glad to get rid of them."

I glanced at Sage, and she shrugged. "We have plenty of room. You can bring them over later."

"I'll leave them on the porch if you're not in. I'll put them in a box so they can't escape."

Sorcha would never dump a box of kittens anywhere. It was a sign she'd been badly affected by whatever was polluting the town.

"Are you still here?" Sorcha pointed out the door to Denver. "Don't let it hit you in the head on your way out. And take a hint. Don't come back. You can tell the other vampires to stay away, too. I know Remus is planning trouble with you and his bunch of psycho fang-heads, and I want nothing to do with it. This is no longer a vampire-friendly place."

Denver gulped, and his gaze dropped to the floor.

Sorcha smirked. "Can you remember all of that, or should I write you a note?"

He heaved out a sigh and nodded. "You won't see me again."

"Thank the stars and moon for that," Sorcha said. "And everybody else, that's your lot. I'm closing for the day."

Customers grumbled, grabbing their takeout bags and mugs and heading out.

"Before we leave, I wanted to ask you about some customers you had in here on the night of the murder," I said.

Sorcha walked to the door and flipped the sign to closed. "I figured you'd be poking about in that. Who are you interested in? A strangling, wasn't it?"

"We believe so. A man called Jim Stool said he brought a date here. She was short and blonde, with feathers tied into the ends of her hair. Does that description sound familiar?"

Sorcha wrinkled her nose. "I've not been that busy. Most people are getting their food and drink at the festival. I'm sure I'd have remembered seeing a woman with feathers in her hair."

"She'd have been with a man of around sixty with a red face tattoo. He's usually wearing dirty jeans and a stained white vest."

"He sounds charming."

"He's Azureus Stool's father," I said. "The victim I found behind the marquee at the festival."

"If you found the body, doesn't that make you a suspect, too?" Sorcha's cold smirk reappeared.

"Fortunately, I have Sage as my alibi."

Sorcha turned away. "I can't confirm that guy and his date were here. He must have lied to you. Now, off you go. I have plans to make."

Given the mood Sorcha was in, there was no point asking more questions, so we hurried outside.

"Do you think Sorcha lied to us or Jim faked his alibi?" Sage asked.

"Sorcha is in a strange head space at the moment, but there's no reason for her to conceal information. She doesn't know Jim or Azureus."

"So Jim is the liar," Sage said. "He gave us a fake alibi because he was at the festival killing his son."

"He remains our prime suspect." I glanced over my shoulder at the café. "I'd hoped a full stomach would clear our heads so we could focus."

"I'm too heartbroken to eat," Sage said. "I like the hollow feeling inside me. It matches my mood."

My stomach grumbled. "There's still food at home. There are also supplies at animal control if we can break in. We won't starve just yet."

"More's the pity," Sage muttered.

"Let's return to Jim's campervan and let him know we've checked his alibi, and it doesn't hold water. It might make him sweat, so he slips up."

"And confesses to the murder. The guy's got 'rat' written all over him. He'll probably try to lay the blame on Reeny's shoulders, though," Sage said.

"I wouldn't put it past him to force Reeny to confess to something he didn't do," I said. "As his master, Jim can order Reeny to do just about anything."

"Let's hope the sniveling little slave has more backbone than he appears to have."

"That's unkind," I said. "From all accounts, Reeny has had a hard life. When you're pushed around, ignored, or told to keep quiet for years, you learn the behavior that keeps you alive."

"What's to say Reeny didn't snap?" Sage trundled beside me, her harness still squeaking. "He must be holding onto anger. All his life, he's been passed around because he wasn't wanted, was overlooked, or told to keep quiet and not have opinions. That can't do his head much good."

"You might be right," I said. "Reeny is a cause for concern."

"Isn't that him?" Sage lifted her chin, and I followed the direction of her gaze. "He's carrying something."

I studied the skinny elf as he scurried away from the festival. "Is he making a run for it? Let's follow him and see what he's doing."

Reeny moved furtively, staying off the main road as much as possible and ducking into alleyways every time he saw someone.

"The little guy's up to something shady," Sage said.

I watched as he pulled papers out of the bag he carried, checked them, and then hid them away again. His head lifted, and he spotted us. For a second, he didn't move, then he took off running, the bag banging against his back.

"That proves he's definitely up to no good!" I looked back at Sage as I chased after Reeny. "Don't stand there! We need to catch him and ask what he's up to."

"You do the running and chasing. I'll do the sitting on the suspect and questioning."

My paws flew as I followed Reeny. He diverted along an alleyway, got to the end, and threw out a spell. Before it took effect, I latched my murder mittens onto his ankle and was flipped into his magic. It was a translocation spell and sucked me along with it, depositing me at the boundary of Crimson Cove.

Reeny yelped and kicked out in an attempt to dislodge me. "Don't hurt me. I've done nothing wrong."

"Then why did you run when you saw us?" My claws remained firmly embedded in his thin calf.

Reeny squirmed in an attempt to get away. "You startled me. You were stalking me. You and that cat on wheels. I got scared."

"We weren't stalking you, but when you acted furtively, we knew something was up. Hold on a moment, let me tell my companion where I am." I sent a blast of magic into the sky, sending silver sparkles down to our location.

A few seconds later, Sage popped into view and shook out her fur. "I lost you in the alley."

"Translocation spell," I said. "I jumped on just in time."

"Is he talking?" She ambled over.

"I promise, I'll tell you everything you want to know," Reeny said. "But I must leave now."

"What's the hurry?" I asked.

Reeny heaved out a quivering sigh. "I've had enough of this family and their demands."

"It can't be easy for you," I said. "But sneaking off isn't the solution."

"Have you checked the bag?" Sage asked.

Reeny clutched the bag and shook his head. "It's my belongings. I only took the basics. I'm not greedy. But I can't be here anymore."

"Sadly, the law is on Jim's side," I said. "If you get caught, you'll be sent back to him. You have a contract."

"Which is why I must go now!" Reeny said. "If I can get a head start, Jim may not even try to find me. He's lazy and lacks motivation."

"You still haven't shown us what's in the bag," Sage said. "It smells funky."

"No! It's my personal things. Stay back." Reeny attempted to scuttle away, but when my claws dug in harder, he squeaked and stopped moving.

"Sage, look in the bag," I said.

Reeny protested, but Sage slashed a claw across the bottom of the bag. A huge heap of pungent smelling dried mushrooms poured out.

Sage stepped back. "It looks like we caught ourselves a killer and a thief all rolled into one."

Chapter 13

Got you

"How... how did that get in there?" Reeny tried to back away again, but with my claws stuck in his skin, he was going nowhere without causing himself an injury.

"You put it there," I said. "You were making a run for it with a stash of stolen fungi."

"No! I mean, I was running, but not for the reason you think. Please, let me go. You can have the mushrooms. I'll figure something else out." Reeny jerked as I tightened my hold on his leg.

"Why steal the fungi?" Sage asked.

Reeny shook and sweated. "I need to earn money. I told you I was paid a pittance by Azureus, and I don't expect Jim to give me anything. He tells me daily I should be grateful I have a position. I'm trapped with him. Unless I flee, I won't have a life worth living."

"You were planning on selling this dried fungi?" I dabbed at a piece of the wrinkled mushroom.

"I have no other resources," Reeny said. "The family I have cares nothing about me. It's impossible to keep a friendship going because I'm always worked so hard. I have no one I can rely on. I needed something to sell to set myself up and start a new life."

"Do you use this stuff?" I asked. "It has unpleasant side effects. I've seen it make people hallucinate and do terrible things."

"Never! I hate it. I prefer to keep a clear head and my feet firmly in reality. And I agree with you. You get the combinations wrong, and it makes people weird."

"Just like everybody in town," Sage said. "It's like they're all eating the stuff."

Tears trickled down Reeny's cheeks. "Please, let me go. I shouldn't have stolen it, but I was desperate. I fear I'll never be free."

"Answer our questions, and we'll consider what to do with you," I said.

Reeny's gaze went to the road that led out of Crimson Cove. "All I want is a quiet life. A family who cares for me and a kind employer. Surely, that's not too much to ask."

"I don't disagree," I said. "And it's wrong you're being forced to work with such an unpleasant man and not being properly paid."

"I can't be his slave," Reeny said. "I've met Jim many times when he's been begging for scraps from Azureus. He has a nasty vibe. He only ever thinks about himself and what he can get out of the situation. He'll make me do things I don't want to do, so he gets a good outcome. This is my only option."

"What about Azureus?" I asked. "You said you respected his work, but you made no comment about the man himself. Was he a difficult employer too?"

Reeny pressed his lips together. "I won't speak badly about him."

"But you want to," I said. "From the clues you've dropped about your working conditions, Azureus didn't think much of you. Since he was content to have you under contract as basically a slave, it suggests a lack of moral decency."

Reeny nodded but said nothing.

"Did you approve of what he did with the fungi?" I asked.

"Azureus had a magical knack with it," Reeny said. "It was as if he was at one with fungi. He said he could tune into the vibrational energies and learn about the fungi properties without even touching it. That was special."

"I work with someone in animal control who uses devices to do a similar thing," I said. "He was excited because he discovered fungi had different vibrational patterns."

"They do! Azureus was a giant conductor of energy that tapped into the magical properties of fungi," Reeny said. "As far as I could tell, he was one-of-a-kind. There are other magic users who have a small amount of ability with fungi, but never anyone with his natural talent. I used to wonder if he was part fungi." He nervously chuckled.

"It sounds like you're telling the truth about Azureus," I said. "You really can't lie?"

"It's highly inadvisable because it causes so much pain," Reeny replied.

"What do you think of my tail?" I asked.

Reeny's forehead furrowed. "I don't understand."

"Is it glorious?"

"It is. It's very fluffy. It must take a lot of work to keep it looking so nice."

"It does. I missed my tail when I didn't have it, but it is time-consuming to deal with. And what about Sage's tail?" I asked.

"Don't drag me into this," Sage said.

"Um... It's a little worn around the edges," Reeny said. "Do you have trouble grooming because of your harness?"

"I groom just fine when I have a mind to," Sage said. "Don't be dissecting my cleaning routine and making assumptions. And I only smell strange because Vorana's not here to give me my regular bath."

Reeny looked confused. "I'm not sure what's going on."

"I was checking if you could lie. Tell us the truth about Azureus," I said.

He heaved out a teary sigh. "You already think I killed him, so anything I say will go against me."

"We need a complete picture of what kind of man he was," I said. "His father had a distorted opinion of Azureus, and those he worked with appear jealous of him. But what did you think of him?"

Reeny dabbed away the tears on his cheeks with the back of his hand. "He was an exacting man. Utterly obsessed with fungi. He wanted everyone to experience its incredible properties. He worked tirelessly to create pure blends of different fungi so people could try them."

"Did he have a license to do that?" Sage asked.

"He could sell anywhere to anyone," Reeny said. "And he did. Azureus had a grand plan, you see, to make connections with world leaders and get them interested in his fungi."

"So he could influence them? Get them hooked on his product and bend them to his will?" I asked. "Azureus was going for world domination through fungi manipulation."

"No. Well, in a way. But only so he could make fungi's magical properties mainstream," Reeny said. "People have strange ideas about fungi. Some belittle it. Some are scared of it. But mainly, people don't understand it. And it must be handled carefully. I've seen what happens when people misuse it. Azureus's father is the perfect example. Overusing the wrong type of mushroom sent him funny. He treats it like it's candy. Fungi is sacred and must be respected. Azureus taught me that."

"That huge plan of his must have kept you busy," I said. "You can't take over the world on your own."

"Azureus worked me hard, and he could be thoughtless rather than cruel. He got so wrapped up in his work that he'd forget about eating and sleeping. Not just for himself, but for others, too."

Given Reeny's statements about our tails and his comments about Azureus, I had to believe he was being honest about not being able to lie. "I'll ask you a straight question. Did you murder Azureus?"

"I promise, I didn't," Reeny said solemnly.

"Was his death an accident?" I asked. "Perhaps Azureus became entangled in rope and you didn't help him get free."

"That also didn't happen," Reeny said. "I was asleep under his campervan. Azureus ordered me to leave him alone because he needed to decompress. It was typical behavior, so I didn't think anything of it. And I was glad of the break. I was exhausted."

"What about Jim?" Sage asked. "Do you think he murdered Azureus?"

"I believe it in my heart. He's crazy enough to do it," Reeny said. "Once you've been around him a few times, you see how cold and unloving he is. Azureus rarely talked about his father, but when he did, there was no affection. It was mainly disappointment that Jim didn't make the effort to become a better parent. We all have our struggles, but it's up to us to recognize when we need to improve and make the difficult changes."

"Change is hard," I said. "People have to reach a crisis point before they make any significant shifts in their lives."

"And that was Jim's problem," Reeny said. "When he hit a brick wall, he'd ask Azureus for help. It was usually a request for special fungi, but sometimes money. Occasionally, a place to stay. Once he got what he wanted, he dropped the good dad act and disappeared. Azureus wanted to love his father, but he made it impossible."

"What about Jim's alibi?" I asked. "He told us he went on a date with a blonde woman who had feathers in her hair. We checked at the café he told us he went to, and the owner couldn't confirm she saw him."

Reeny looked away.

"You have to tell us the truth," I said.

"Unless Jim has forbidden you to," Sage said. "Can he do that?"

"He can force orders on me," Reeny said. "But he hasn't in relation to this information. Jim always brags about his conquests. It's distasteful. I just don't want to answer in case it means he's in the clear. I want Jim to go away for a long time, so I don't have to deal with him."

"Does that mean you know about this woman he took on a date?" I asked.

Reeny stared down at the mound of fungi. "He's met several women since he's been here. And there was a blonde lady with feathers in her hair."

"Did Jim take her out on the night Azureus was murdered?" I asked.

Reeny didn't speak for a long minute. "He did. I got left behind."

"Do you know the lady's name?" Sage asked.

"Florence Crystal. She's staying in a small pink tent with a feathered dreamcatcher outside. If she's still here, she should be easy to find."

This new information, unfortunately, meant Jim was most likely innocent. "Don't leave Crimson Cove. We may have more questions for you."

"But I'm not safe! I can't go back to Jim. If he discovers I attempted to leave, he'll be cruel. I fear for my life."

"There's plenty of room at our place," Sage said. "There are places to sleep and food. You can crash with us until you figure something out."

More tears appeared. "You'd really help me?"

"We'd be happy to," I said. And with Reeny locked in our house, he'd be less able to flee. I was almost a hundred percent convinced he was innocent, but I needed to be sure he'd pose no more problems for us.

Reeny lurched forward and hugged us, causing Sage to hiss and back away. "Thank you. I'm so rarely shown kindness that it feels alien."

"It's just a house," Sage said. "And the food is basic."

Reeny sighed. "It's so much more than that."

We led a weeping, smiling Reeny swiftly to Vorana's house, settled him in with food, showed him the guest bedroom, and then carefully locked the doors and placed a ward around the house so he couldn't escape.

"What do you make of the little dude?" Sage asked as we headed back to the campsite to find Florence.

"He's had a tough life. Perhaps we can find a way to get him out of his contract. All contracts can be broken if you know which law to bend."

"If we get Jim arrested for illegally dealing fungi, that would get him off Reeny's back," Sage said. "Jim goes to jail, and Reeny is free."

"I like your thinking," I said. "When we have a moment, we'll pursue that idea."

After twenty minutes of searching the campsite, avoiding the raucous fungi revelers and impromptu parties, we discovered a small pink tent with a feathered dreamcatcher outside. The flaps were unzipped, and a quick peek inside revealed a scantily dressed blonde lady munching on a cereal bar.

She jumped when she saw me looking in but then waved. "Hello, cutie. What can I do for you?"

I winced at her high, squeaky voice. "Greetings! I'm Juno, and this is my friend, Sage. Do you mind if we ask you a few questions?"

"I've got nothing happening for an hour, so I'm all yours. Are you here for the festival?"

"We live in town," Sage said. "We're investigating the recent murder."

Florence swallowed her mouthful of cereal bar. "You mean the guy found strangled behind the marquee? Everyone was talking about that. I thought it had been dealt with, though. The angels caught someone, didn't they?"

"Sadly, not yet," I said. "We're interested in a man you may know."

Her eyes widened. "For the murder?"

"Possibly."

"Then you're looking in the wrong place, sweetie pie. I only date good guys. I've learned that the hard way."

"You didn't go on a date with Jim Stool to a café in town on the night of the murder?" I asked.

"Jim! Well, I did." Florence finished her cereal bar and opened a small brown bag full of chocolate truffle treats. "That one had me fooled. He behaved like an angel when we met. He told me he was looking for something serious after being widowed.

I believed his sob story and thought he was charming."

"What changed your mind about him?" I asked.

"Jim took me to this cute café, and we ordered dinner. It was going well, but he got distracted by someone. I couldn't see who it was, but he kept looking away from me, and I had to keep repeating my questions. I should have given up on him then," Florence said.

"Go on," I said.

"After a couple of minutes, Jim excused himself to go to the bathroom. I didn't think it was strange, and I was happy to sit and soak in the vibes while I waited for the food. But after ten minutes and he hadn't returned, I got worried."

"You went looking for Jim?"

Florence nodded. "I went to the bathroom, opened the door, and discovered him locking lips with some mushroom tart."

"We're not talking a literal mushroom tart here, are we?"

Florence chuckled. "Sadly not. Some floozy half his age and wearing barely any clothes. She had a mushroom-shaped backpack and wore a dress with mushroom sparkles all over it. Super tacky."

"Who was it?" I asked.

"I had no idea and no interest in finding out. I grabbed a bar of soap, flung it at his head, and left the café. I wasn't wasting my time on that loser."

"What time did you leave the café?" I asked.

"We were eating late. We got there before the festival ended, but it was winding up. It must have been around about eight thirty that evening. Maybe nine."

"Did you come back to your tent?" I asked.

"No, I went for a walk to calm down."

"Did Jim follow you?"

"He was sensible enough not to bother. He most likely stayed in the bathroom and finished what he'd started. Dirty dog." Florence snitched her nose and popped a large truffle into her mouth.

This information put Jim in the clear. He had been at Sorcha's café with Florence and a mystery woman. That meant he was innocent of murder.

"Do you reckon Jim did it?" Florence leaned closer, her eyes bright with interest and possibly whatever was in her magical truffles. "Did I almost have dinner with a killer?"

"No, we just needed to check his alibi," I said.

"It would have served him right if you did arrest him." Florence offered us a mushroom truffle, but we both declined. "He's a bad guy. No one likes a cheater."

"Unless they come with fur and spots. Enjoy the rest of your festival," I said.

We left the tent and hurried away.

Sage yawned loudly. "So it wasn't the dad. Bad luck for us. If it had been Jim, we could have solved this and then slept for a week."

"Sadly, no rest for us just yet. Let's check on Gilly and Kinoko next."

Sage yawned again. "Tomorrow. All this hunting around and asking questions is exhausting. I'm not used to it."

I was tired too. I hadn't cat napped, and although it was early, rest and recovery sounded like the right idea.

"We'll return home and check on Reeny," I said. "We'll continue our adventure in the morning."

Sage groaned. "We should frame Jim. He deserves it. Everyone we speak to about him describes him as a scummy guy. Let's get a scumbag off the streets."

I gently head-butted my exhausted companion. "That's not how justice works. Tomorrow is a new day, with new clues, more delving, and even better crime solving."

We were almost home when Sage stopped. "Something is hissing. Is it a snake?"

I cocked my head then sighed as my gaze landed on a box on the porch. "Something much deadlier than a snake."

Chapter 14

Double surprise

"If you bite me again, I'm rehoming you." I shook my head to dislodge the needle teeth attempting to pierce my soft ear.

"That wasn't me," Sage muttered, half asleep.

"I know! These three haven't stopped bothering me all night." I placed a paw on top of one of the kittens' heads as he attempted to pounce on Sage. It would end badly if Sage was disturbed from her slumber by an overly excited feral kitten looking to play. Or bite. Or savage.

After discovering the dumped kittens on the porch without even a note or any food for them, all hopes of cat naps and restorative snacks had gone out the window, as I'd dealt with the three rambunctious babies. They were tiny tornadoes of magical energy, bouncing around, sparking spells they didn't understand, and delighting every time they set fire to something.

And I'd been the one attempting to control them. Sage had washed her paws of the kittens and lumbered up to Vorana's bedroom to sleep, with a clear message of 'do not disturb' as she slammed the door.

She had, however, relented, so we'd all slept in the same room. Although she'd not been any help. Once Sage was in a deep sleep, a magnitude ten earthquake wouldn't rouse her.

"What's that smell?" I asked.

"That also wasn't me," Sage said. "Although I am feeling gassy. I can't promise something won't pop out if I make any sudden moves."

"No! It's a pleasant smell. Almost like savory pancakes."

That got Sage's head lifting. She inhaled deeply and her eyes shot open. "Vorana is back! She must be making us breakfast." She rolled off the bed and hit the floor, temporarily forgetting her back legs didn't work.

I peered over the edge of the bed as the kittens yanked on my tail. "Take it steady. You don't want to alarm the babies."

The kittens seemed enchanted by Sage's sudden action as they zoomed to the edge of the bed and looked at her with wide, excited eyes, preparing to jump.

"Help me into my harness," Sage said. "I must see Vorana."

"Don't get too excited. It may not be her."

"Who else makes such delicious smells that waft up from the kitchen? Get out of my way. I'm going to see my witch."

Before I could remind Sage we had an obedient house-elf hiding in our home, she was gone in a clatter of metal harness and scrabbling claws.

I collected the kittens, ensuring they were safely secured on my back, before heading down the stairs.

As predicted, it wasn't Vorana back from her adventures. Reeny had pulled a stool over to the stove and stood on it, one of Vorana's flowered aprons around his thin waist. He was flipping pancakes as I entered the kitchen.

"It's only him," Sage said on a growl. "I forgot we had a guest."

"I feared you may have," I said. "But look on the bright side. At least we get a delicious breakfast. No more foraging and attempting to get access to tins without an opener."

Sage grunted and slumped over to her prickly mat by the back door. She sat staring at the door, hunched into a small ball of despair.

"Did I do something wrong?" Reeny asked, holding the pancake flipper above the pan. "I wanted to treat you. You've been so kind, giving me shelter and a warm place to sleep. I thought that was it for me when you caught me leaving town, but now I have a home."

"A temporary home," Sage groused. "Don't get too comfortable."

Reeny's smile faded. "I promise not to overstay my welcome. I'll leave the second you tell me to. I travel light since I have few personal possessions, so I can be out of here in three minutes. Maybe less if I run."

"There's no need to go anywhere." I nudged one of the kittens back onto my shoulder. "And your breakfast is a welcome surprise. As you may have noticed from the depleted pantry, things are a little odd around here."

"Is it just the two of you living here?" Reeny returned to flipping the pancakes. "It's a big place for two cats."

"We live here with our bonded magic users," I said. "They're on an extended vacation."

"Abandoned us, you mean," Sage grumbled.

Reeny looked at me with surprise in his eyes, but I shook my head. I didn't want to encourage Sage to get any sulkier.

"I hope there's plenty of food. As you can see, these kittens need feeding up," I said.

"They're delightful, if a little scary." Reeny watched as I extinguished a tiny fireball. "Don't worry. There's enough to feed a small army. And I love to cook for people. It's a way I show my gratitude and fondness."

"Does that mean you never cook for Jim?" Sage asked.

"He's more of a takeout guy," Reeny said. "But if he ordered me to, I'd cook for him. It may not be the most delicious meal I'd ever made, though. Shall we sit at the breakfast table?"

"We've been more casual since our witches disappeared," I said. "So it'll make a nice change to sit at the table. What do you think, Sage?"

"You can do what you like. I'm eating here."

"At least you're eating," I murmured. "The kittens can run about on the table safely, too. I can eat and watch them."

"When you came in yesterday, you didn't say how you came about these kittens." Reeny dashed around, setting the table for us.

"Someone in town fosters strays," I said. "She's been distracted recently, so I'm looking after the kittens until she has more time to devote to them."

"I'm not an expert in all forms of magic, but I can see how powerful they are," Reeny said. "Are you sure they're safe?"

"Not entirely, but I've got a handle on things." I yanked my tail out of one of the kitten's mouths. "Shall we eat?"

Even though I attempted to get Sage to join us at the table, she stubbornly refused, so Reeny placed a plate of pancakes beside her, so she could enjoy them from the discomfort of her prickly mat.

I cast a ward spell over the kittens, so it was impossible for them to fall off the table and injure themselves, before settling down with a huge stack of delicious-looking savory pancakes served by Reeny. He served himself a single pancake and one slice of apple.

"You can eat more if you want to," I said.

"I never have much of an appetite," Reeny said. "But you enjoy yourselves. I get pleasure out of watching people eat my food."

"He's a feeder," Sage said from around a huge mouthful of pancake.

"That works for me." I bit into the buttery rich pancake and instantly got a delicious tang of smoke and meat. "What's in these?"

"I had to improvise, since you didn't have all the ingredients. I mixed in beef stock and barbecue sauce. I hope they're acceptable."

"They're perfection," I said. "Thank you, Reeny."

"I live to serve." He blushed. "And I do enjoy it when I have a decent master. Sadly, those have been lacking lately."

I finished my mouthful and nudged a kitten away from Reeny's slice of apple. "You'll be sad to know Jim is no longer a suspect. We found Florence, and she confirmed she went to the café with Jim on the night of the murder. She left without him, because she caught him in the bathroom with another woman."

"How unpleasant for her," Reeny said. "And how typical of Jim to have no regard for anyone but himself."

"Florence mentioned the woman was much younger than Jim and described her as a mushroom tart. She said her dress had mushroom sparkles on it. Does that ring any bells with you?"

"Nearly everyone is wearing something at this festival that is fungi related," Reeny said. "I've seen hundreds of women in pretty mushroom dresses. Some even wear mushroom-shaped hats. I find it bizarre."

"At least there are no mushrooms in these pancakes," Sage said. "They always taste like warm slugs."

"They have a particular texture that takes getting used to," I said. "I'd be interested in knowing more about this younger woman. Surely, Jim couldn't have just met her and decided to have naughty fun in the bathroom."

"He picks women who have... an expandable set of morals," Reeny said. "Perhaps that's the prude in me coming out, but if a woman ever mentions getting serious with him and wanting a steady relationship, he bolts."

"Has Jim had a lot of relationships?" I asked.

"I wouldn't call them relationships." Reeny's gaze was eager and focused as I consumed his delicious pancakes. "The man has an inability to keep it in his pants, and he's always chasing after someone. He used to brag about it with Azureus."

"What did Azureus think about that?"

"He was embarrassed. He told his father several times to grow up." Reeny nibbled on his apple. "This is sad news. I'm still Jim's slave if he's innocent of murder."

"He is, but we're looking at other ways to get him out of your life. Don't give up hope. If we can figure it out, you won't have to be a slave to that family anymore."

Reeny busied himself with his napkin, but I didn't miss the shimmer of tears in his eyes. I was happy I could bring a small amount of joy to this lonely elf's life.

"We're visiting Gilly and Kinoko today," I said. "We wondered if they had anything to do with what happened to Azureus. Neither of them were complimentary about him."

"They wouldn't be. But murdering someone would take away everything they'd worked so hard for." Reeny pulled apart his pancake. "Have you met Azureus's girlfriend?"

"Selena showed up at Angel Force." I nudged a bouncy kitten away from the table edge. "At first, we thought she was distraught because Azureus died, but she behaved much like his father. She wanted to know what happened to him and then informed us she was the main beneficiary of Azureus's will and wanted his personal effects."

"That's hardly a surprise." Reeny peered at the bouncing kitten with a hint of alarm in his eyes. "Jim and Selena are cut from the same cloth."

"Do you know how serious things were between Azureus and Selena?"

"He'd known Selena from a young age and had asked her out dozens of times, but she only got interested once he became famous and made his fortune. She also liked the free fungi Azureus gave out." Reeny grimaced. "She wasn't in that relationship for love. She was nasty. Out for what she could get and nothing more."

"Is there a lot of money to be made from selling fungi?" I asked.

"Plenty of money if you have the right skills. Does that kitten need the bathroom? It won't stop bouncing."

I scooped up the kitten and made a hole in the protective ward so he could go outside. "Behave. And come right back."

The kitten shot away, and I returned to the table.

Reeny looked at my almost empty plate. "Fungi is extraordinarily special. And depending on the type of fungi used, it's incredibly strong. It could knock out the most powerful magic user."

"Why would you want to knock someone out?" My tongue suddenly felt too large for my mouth, and my vision glazed.

Reeny hopped off his seat as the world tilted. "I'm so sorry, but you don't know how truly terrible Jim is. He destroys people for fun. And I don't know either of you, so you may be being honest with me, but I can't take that risk."

"What's happening?" At least, I think that's what I said. My eyes were heavy, and my brain had slowed to a crawl.

"It'll do you no harm. You'll sleep and then wake up. And once again, I really am sorry. You do seem like nice magic users, but over the years, I've lost all trust. I must look after myself while I have this opportunity."

Reeny was saying something else, but the words made no sense as I sank into a deep darkness.

❧ ☙

A sharp pain in my ear roused me. I blinked bleary eyes to discover a kitten was using my ear as a chew toy. I rolled away, but the kitten came with me, so I gently shoved him off with a paw.

"No more chewing!" I winced at how loud my voice sounded.

Another kitten jumped on my head, meowing deafeningly at me, almost causing me to pass out as pain stabbed through my skull.

I flopped onto my belly. I must have fallen off the chair because I was on the kitchen floor. My gaze went to the prickly mat, and I was relieved to see Sage softly snoring.

"Stop attacking me and help Sage," I said to the relentless kittens. "She needs a jolt to get her awake."

The kittens leapt into action, tumbling over themselves in their eagerness to bite Sage and leap all over her.

"Gently," I cautioned. "In her advanced age, she doesn't need sudden shocks to the system."

It appeared the kittens didn't know what the word 'gentle' meant. One jumped on Sage's head, another on her back, and the male landed on her tail.

Sage shrieked and reared up, batting away one of the kittens. There were a few seconds of fearsome hissing from all sides, which I allowed as I composed my thoughts and ensured the world wasn't rocking too badly. My tongue still felt gross, and my stomach churned. Reeny had deceived us.

"Will you get these tiny monsters away from me?" Sage hissed again. "Why did you set them upon me?"

"Because we're facing trouble and must be alert," I said. "Do you remember what happened?"

Sage batted away one of the kittens again as it made a lunge for her ear. "We were eating breakfast. It was delicious."

"And then?"

"Then... I woke up to this." Sage growled at the smallest kitten, who was fearless in its pursuit of her tail.

"You don't remember feeling odd?" I asked. "We passed out! That wasn't a natural sleep. Reeny put something in our food to knock us out."

Sage inhaled sharply. "I remember feeling lightheaded. I thought it was because I wasn't breathing properly after inhaling so much food. I couldn't get enough of Reeny's pancakes. That little jerk really drugged us?"

"You don't see him here, do you?" I stumbled to the door and shoved my paw through the gap I'd made in the magic ward. It was big enough for a skinny elf to squeeze through. "And he didn't touch the only pancake on his plate. He nibbled at an apple. Reeny wasn't repaying our kindness. He'd planned an escape."

"Why? If he's innocent of murder, there's no reason to run from us." Sage spat at the kittens as they formed a semi-circle in front of her, determined to have their fun.

"Reeny needed to get away from Jim." I groaned as my stomach flipped over. "We need a swift cure for this problem, and I know of only one thing to deal with this immediately."

Sage grunted. "A gross grass purge."

"It's what the best cats do to get rid of a stomach upset. And the kittens need fresh air and a comfort break. We've been out for hours."

Sage swiped at the circling kittens. "I hate grass purges."

"It's good for the colon. Let's get it over with. Once we can think clearly, we'll figure out how to deal with Reeny." Rather than attempt to fumble with the kitchen door handle, I used a spell to open it. The fearless kittens bundled out, thinking it was a game, while I struggled out with Sage and over to the nearest patch of rich green, damp grass. "Five mouthfuls each. That'll do the job."

Sage grunted and complained with every mouthful, but in less than a minute, the contents of our stomachs glistened on the grass. My thoughts were no longer muddled, and my tongue felt the correct size for my mouth.

"I swear eternal revenge on that house-elf," Sage said. "Did Reeny drug us because he's a killer? Did he get around his inability to lie and fool us both?"

"To figure that out, we must find him," I said. "And he's got a good eight-hour head start."

"Try a location spell. I don't care where he is. I'm taking him down," Sage said.

I kept an eye on the kittens as I cast the spell. "Huh. That can't be right."

"What do you see?"

"It's showing Reeny is still in Crimson Cove. He's gone back to the festival."

"I figured he'd run for it," Sage said. "He must have gone back to get more fungi. I'm gonna pound that slippery sucker into the dirt."

"Give me five minutes to deal with the kittens, and then we'll get him," I said.

"Obliteration time?" Sage smashed a paw in the dirt.

I nodded. "Obliteration time."

Chapter 15

Festival fun

We were back at the festival, dodging overexcited revelers and getting our tails trodden on repeatedly. There was a strange, musky, rotten smell in the air, suggesting a stallholder hadn't properly stored their produce. Whatever the stench was, it made me wrinkle my booping snooter and take shallow breaths.

"How will we find Reeny in all this chaos?" Sage swiped a paw at a man who almost trod on her, causing him to yelp and jump away. "There are more people here than the last time we came."

"Word must be spreading about the festival," I said.

"Everyone wants a piece of the magical mushroom action," Sage said. "I don't get it."

The atmosphere at the festival had shifted from fun to tense. Several fights broke out as we continued through the crowd, looking for Reeny. People were no longer having fun. They were looking for trouble and easily finding it.

"I'll try another location spell, see if we can narrow down to a particular section of the festival." I threw out the spell. The magic sparkled in the air and was settling on a spot when someone walked through the spell, dispersing it.

"We need to find somewhere quieter," Sage said. "If anyone else bumps into me or treads on my tail, I'll go nuclear."

It took a few minutes of searching, but we finally ducked behind a marquee where nobody lurked. I cast the spell again.

"He's not that far from here." Sage peered at the white dot that hovered in front of us.

"I'm still surprised Reeny came back to the festival," I said. "He doesn't strike me as a risk-taker, and he must know the second we woke, we'd pursue him."

"Perhaps he was hoping we wouldn't wake," Sage said. "He drugged us with something powerful, thinking it would kill us. But we beat it."

"He underestimated us if he thought he could kill us with some of his funky fungi. Let's follow the dot and see where it leads us."

"He's not moving!" Sage kept checking the dot. "He's probably found a stash of fungi and is loading up before vanishing."

"Reeny must be desperate if he thinks he can get away with this," I said. "And why has it taken him so long to grab more fungi and flee? We've been passed out all day."

"Who cares? He's a weasel, and we're taking him out."

As best we could, we kept to the edge of the festival, skirting behind marquees whenever there was room. Even when we did, we'd often come across canoodling couples or large piles of trash that we couldn't clamber over.

"I see angels!" Sage said. "Should we tell them what's going on?"

Cythera was dancing in a circle of angels, her wings spread wide and an uncharacteristic smile on her face, her mouth smeared with chocolate and a drink in her hand.

"They won't have any interest in what we're doing," I said. "We're on our own."

We continued following the dot, getting ever closer. Reeny was still in the same spot. He hadn't moved an inch. What was he doing?

"There he is!" Sage shot off, and I followed.

Reeny wasn't loading up with fungi. He was peering around the corner of a marquee, suggesting he was watching somebody. We were almost on top of him when he turned and spotted us. He yelped in surprise and dashed away.

We pursued, weaving among the crowd and, when necessary, blasting people out of our way with spells.

"Reeny, stop!" I yelled. "You know you're in trouble. You won't get away with this."

Reeny's small size was in his favor as he dodged around people, and I almost lost sight of him.

"I'll whack him with a spell to bring him down," Sage said.

"Be careful not to hit anyone else," I said.

"They're all too high to care if they get whacked with one of my spells." Sage took aim and fired.

The spell skimmed off Reeny's shoulder. He staggered but stayed on his feet and kept running.

"He's a slippery little sneak," Sage said.

"He's a terrified little sneak. He knows what we'll do to him when we catch up."

"He's got to be guilty of killing Azureus," Sage said. "You don't drug people and run if you're innocent."

"Which means he lied about his ability to tell untruths." I leaped over a smooching couple who were rolling around in the dirt.

"So he's our killer," Sage said.

"With Jim's alibi confirmed, it's got to be Reeny. Let's catch him and get a confession."

Reeny zigzagged through the crowded festival, darting between revelers. He vaulted over a picnic table, scattering plates and cups, while people shouted in surprise. I pushed off the ground, launching after him, my paws barely touching the table before I sprang forward.

Sage was right behind me.

Reeny glanced back, his eyes wide with fear, and then plunged headfirst into a cluster of children playing some kind of oversized mushroom hat game, passing the hats around as they chanted.

I skidded to a halt, narrowly avoiding a collision with a little girl holding a giant brown cotton candy. Sage, less graceful, barreled into the candy, leaving a sticky brown smear across her fur. She shook herself off and kept going, her eyes locked on Reeny's fleeing form.

Reeny dove between two food stalls, the smell of fried dough and roasted mushrooms mingling in the air. He knocked over a stack of crates, sending candied mushrooms tumbling into our path. I leaped over the mushrooms, barely maintaining my balance as I landed and kept running.

Sage plowed through, her claws scrabbling for purchase.

The space opened up into a stage filled with jugglers, stilt-walkers, and acrobats. Reeny darted through the performers. He scrambled up the side of a stage, knocking over a prop mushroom in his haste.

I followed, my muscles burning with the effort. Sage leaped onto the stage beside me. Reeny jumped down from the other side, landing in a pile of hay that cushioned his fall. He scrambled to his feet and took off again, leaving a trail of scattered hay behind him.

We chased him through a maze of colorful tents. Reeny slipped through a narrow gap between two tents, and I squeezed after him, my fur brushing against the fabric. Sage took a wider route, bursting out from behind a tent and cutting off Reeny's path.

He slid to a stop, his eyes darting left and right. He spotted an opening and sprinted toward it. Reeny vaulted over a fence, his legs pumping furiously as he hit the ground running.

I cleared the fence in a single bound, my heart pounding. We were on a pathway lined with mushroom shaped lanterns that looked like they'd be part of some evening event. Reeny was a blur of motion. He sprinted down the path, his breath coming in ragged gasps, and then veered off into another cluster of stalls.

We were hot on his heels, dodging past bewildered festival-goers. Sage was relentlessly keeping up, her fury-filled eyes never leaving Reeny.

Reeny bolted toward another stage, where a band was performing. He slipped behind the stage, disappearing from view for a moment. I followed, ducking under the stage's wooden supports and emerging on the other side. Reeny was already climbing up the scaffolding, his hands clutching at the metal bars.

I scrambled after him, the metal cool and slippery under my paws. Sage's claws clicked against the scaffolding as she climbed, using magic to support her harness.

Reeny reached the top and leaped onto the roof of a nearby tent, the fabric sagging under his weight. He rolled to his feet and kept running.

"How does he have so much energy?" Sage heaved in a breath.

"Fear and adrenaline. But he's flagging. We've almost got him," I said.

We reached the roof of the tent and sprinted across it, the fabric undulating beneath our paws. Reeny jumped to the next tent, the gap between them yawning like a chasm. I leaped, my heart in my throat as I soared through the air.

I landed hard, the impact jarring my bones, but I didn't slow. Sage landed beside me. Reeny was running out of tents, his path leading him toward the edge of the festival grounds.

He glanced back, but still wasn't giving up. He reached the last tent and leaped off, his arms flailing as he hit the ground and rolled.

"If Reeny gets in the trees, we could lose him," I yelled.

"No, we won't." Sage blasted out a spell, and it slammed into Reeny's back, taking him down.

We zoomed over to him, leaving behind the hectic chaos amid the marquees and stalls.

"It's the end of the line, Reeny," I puffed out as I caught up with him and slammed a paw into his back to stop him from moving.

"I'm sorry!" Reeny stammered out. "I had to prove Jim was guilty of murder. I know he did this."

"We don't believe you anymore," I said.

"Why not? I've only been kind to you," Reeny said. "I made you breakfast."

"You drugged us with that breakfast," I said.

Reeny cringed away. "I knew you wouldn't let me leave that house. And I didn't hurt you."

"Drugging someone is hurting them," Sage said. "How do we know you weren't planning on killing us with whatever you put in that food?"

"Never! But I had to get to the bottom of this."

"We've done that for you. You're guilty, and you didn't want to get caught." Sage swiped a paw at Reeny. "You killed Azureus, and you lied to us. We gave you a roof over your head and protection. This is how you repay us?"

"Easy, my friend," I said. Reeny was a quivering mess, almost choking on his tears and fear.

"There you are!" Jim jogged over, looking as disheveled as ever. "I knew that was you sprinting past the mushroom smoke tent. Where have you been hiding?"

"Help me," Reeny whispered to me. "I can't go back to him. I won't survive."

"Then you shouldn't have drugged us and fled the house." I turned to Jim. "We need to take Reeny in for questioning."

"Questioning about what?" Jim grabbed the back of Reeny's tunic and pulled him to his feet. "I don't expect to have to look for my servant. You should be there, waiting to fulfill my every need before I even know what those needs are. What are you playing at?"

"I want no trouble," Reeny mumbled.

Jim roughly shook Reeny. "You've found it. I don't know how Azureus treated you, but it'll be different with me. You don't go anywhere unless I tell you to. You follow all my orders. You belong to me now, got it?"

Reeny turned his tear-filled eyes to me and nodded. "I always obey my master."

"As charming as it is to see you treat your employees so well," I said, "we need to speak to Reeny. He's a suspect in Azureus's murder."

"A suspect! Don't make me laugh," Jim said. "The only thing he is, is my property. He's not a person, so he can't be accused of anything. Besides, as you can see, he's terrified of his own shadow. Least likely killer on this planet."

"Does that mean you're involved?" I asked Jim.

"Involved in what?"

"Azureus's murder," I said. "It's often a family member who commits the crime. Did you sneak out of the café to murder your own son?"

"Wait a moment. Hold on now. Don't make up stories you can't prove." Jim dropped his hold on Reeny and took a step away.

"We'll get the proof," Sage said. "Maybe you ordered Reeny to commit the murder. And since he's your property, that makes you as guilty as he is because he can't disobey you."

Jim shoved Reeny away and scowled at him. "If this loser killed my son, I'm not going down for the murder. I won't be responsible for what he does when I'm not around."

"If you can't control your property, then it's your fault," I said. "And my genius friend has a point. Who's to say you didn't insist Reeny hurt Azureus?"

"I'm the genius friend, right?" Sage murmured.

"Always."

"Because Reeny despises me," Jim said. "He didn't think much of Azureus either, but he loathes me more. I wouldn't have been able to get him to do anything for me until he became my property."

"One of you did it," Sage said. "Whoever talks first and points the finger will be in less trouble."

Reeny gave a raspy sob. "It wasn't me."

"You be quiet," Jim said. "Don't think you can get rid of me by accusing me of murder. I had nothing to do with it. I came to the festival to get what was due. With the boy dead, my regular supply is cut off."

"And of course, you've lost a much-loved child," I said. "I can see how devastated you are about that."

Jim smirked. "Just because we were related by blood doesn't mean we liked each other or treated each other well. Azureus was clear about what he thought of me. I was an embarrassment. But it cuts both ways. Maybe I was embarrassed by him. I wanted a son who was a real man, not some geek who went camping on weekends to dig up truffles and take photographs of them. What kind of loser does that?"

"The kind of loser you were happy to exploit when he made his fame and fortune with that geeky fungi," I said.

"You can think what you like, but I didn't do it. And I don't think this idiot did either." Jim grabbed hold of Reeny. "Let's get out of here. They've got nothing on us."

"I don't want to go with you," Reeny said.

Jim swiped him around the head. "I don't care what you want or what you need. You belong to me. Keep your mouth shut and move."

As they walked away, I smacked Jim in the butt with a stinging spell, making him yell and whip around.

"Was that you?" He strode back toward me, dragging Reeny beside him.

"Uh-oh. Now you've done it," Sage said.

"Treat Reeny better," I said to Jim. "He may belong to you, but that doesn't mean you have to be cruel."

"Keep out of my business." Jim narrowed his gaze at me. "Or are we going to have a problem?"

"We have a problem," Sage said. "We don't like you. You're mean to Reeny, even though he's a jerk, and you abused your relationship with your son. You also possibly killed him."

"And what are you going to do about it, wheels?" Jim asked. "Run me over?"

"Teach you a lesson you'll never forget," Sage said. "A lesson you may not even walk away from."

Jim chortled and rubbed his hands together. "Don't make promises you can't keep. And you'll be the one who can't walk away, especially not when I've crushed that harness."

Jim and Sage glared at each other, neither of them blinking, the tension flaring.

"Should we do something?" Reeny whispered to me. "Jim uses horrible magic. It really hurts when it hits you."

"Sage can hold her own," I murmured. "Your master is a bully, and I don't expect he's used to people standing up to him."

"I never do," Reeny said. "I'm too scared."

"Baby cakes, what are you doing over here?" Azureus's girlfriend, Selena, stumbled over in ridiculously high heels, her dress just skimming the tops of her thighs. "One minute, we were looking at those mushroom-shaped crystals and inhaling that yummy mushroom smoke, and then you were gone."

"Just dealing with a bit of business," Jim said, not taking his eyes off Sage. "I'll join you soon. Go back to the crystals. Pick one you like. On me."

Selena planted a big kiss on his lips. "Come with me and look at them, you gorgeous creature. I just found out there'll be a mushroom moon soon. It'll be the perfect time for you to make an honest woman out of me."

Chapter 16

Love triangle

Jim pushed Selena away so roughly she almost fell off her heels, a flare of embarrassment coloring his cheeks as his dirty little secret was exposed.

"Hey! Why did you shove me?" Selena scowled at Jim. "You'd better not be hiding another woman around here. We've had that conversation, and you said you're mine. No more skirt."

Jim scrubbed at the back of his neck and glanced my way. "Very funny. Off you go now. Find a crystal you like, and I'll treat you."

Selena stood her ground and crossed her arms over her chest, emphasizing her already ample charms. "I'm going nowhere until you tell me what's going on."

"Excuse me for interrupting this charming exchange," I said, "but are you dating Jim?"

Selena flicked a glance my way. "You're the angel cat, aren't you? The one I met at the station."

"The very same. Although some would say I'm not always considered angelic. Are you two in a relationship?"

"Oh, sugar, it's nothing exclusive. These are modern times. A woman doesn't have to settle for one man."

"So you settled for Azureus and Jim? Azureus's father?" Sage asked.

"Why not? Don't you think they look similar? And I needed to make sure I'd be with a handsome older man if I stayed with Azureus. Jim is so dreamy when he makes an effort." Selena's gaze moved over Jim's disheveled appearance. "Although you haven't been making much of an effort lately. Are you going off me?"

Jim's chuckle sounded awkward. "This is just a bit of fun. Don't go getting any ideas in those furry heads. This has nothing to do with what happened to Azureus."

"You can imagine I'm having one or two ideas," I said. "You were with your son's girlfriend on the night of the murder?"

"No! No labels on any relationships," Selena said. "I'm a free woman. And I won't be judged for my choices."

"You have to be a little judged," Sage said. "What do you see in this guy?"

"Hey! I have assets, and I'm fun," Jim said. "Why wouldn't Selena want to be with me?"

"Because you're a lousy dealer who exploited your son to get what you wanted," Sage said.

"Watch your mouth, wheels. I'm not done with you yet," Jim growled out.

I stepped forward. "How long has this relationship been going on?"

"We've been hopelessly in lust for almost two years," Selena said. "Jim keeps promising he'll marry me, not that I believe in any of that ball and chain nonsense. But with the mushroom moon about to burst out, it'll be the perfect opportunity to have a lavish celebration. Here we are, surrounded by everything magical mushroom, and we can have the ceremony of our dreams. And then a huge party afterward."

"I like the sound of the party," Jim said, "but I never promised to marry you."

"You did! Just the other night when we were in bed. As you were falling asleep, I said to you, 'Jim, baby, it's time you claimed me. I want a ring on my finger and a big party.' And what did you say?"

"I was probably asleep. You always wear me out."

She tittered. "I love an older guy. Some people say I have daddy issues."

"More like sugar daddy issues," Sage whispered to me. "Although there's not much sugar to be found on this daddy. More like crusty decay."

"Let's put aside whether you're getting married soon and if you even believe in the ceremony," I said. "Jim, you must have known Azureus was involved with Selena and that he'd liked her for a long time, but you got together with her, anyway?"

"Like the lady said, nobody was exclusive. Everybody deserves to enjoy themselves, and she's a heck of a good-looking woman."

"You're too kind, baby-boo." Selena fluttered her lashes. "And I know you're only teasing when you say you won't make me an honest woman. I'm the perfect catch. Any man would be proud to have me on their arm. Azureus was. He proposed several times, but I told him I wasn't ready. In truth, I was waiting for the right proposal from the right man."

"Even though you don't believe in marriage?" Sage asked.

Selena shrugged. "I know what I want."

"Jim is your version of the right man?" I couldn't hide the shock from my voice. "Are your expectations set so low?"

"Lots of women like the rough and rugged type," Jim said. "I'm a fantasy."

"Do you mean nightmare?"

"Oh, no! I adore a bit of rough," Selena said. "I even read in a magazine that it's the top fantasy all women have."

"Then they need some serious therapy," Sage whispered to me.

Selena shoved Jim's shoulder. "Now, stop fooling around. I've provisionally booked a venue. It's a little place close by. We can get the food and flowers here and all the edible mushrooms we want. We'll splurge since it's our special union day."

"No union. It's too formal. I like you because you don't want to get hitched. Let's do something else," Jim said.

Selena shoved him again. "I want a ceremony, a ring, and a party. I also want to know what's going on. You're up to something sneaky with these cats and your timid little elf. I don't want anyone else in on our deals."

"What deals?" I pounced on Selena's words.

"We're doing nothing, babe. Just a big misunderstanding. Everybody was just leaving," Jim said. "Let's go see about those crystals. Maybe inhale some more smoke and get your mind off the wedding."

"The only place we're going is Angel Force," I said. "We need to unpick this issue."

"I'm going nowhere with you," Jim said. "You're not law enforcement."

"We are at the moment," I said. "And I'm happy to make a kittizen's arrest."

"Try it," Jim said.

"I hoped you'd say that." Sage shot out a spell that smacked Jim on the side of the head.

He lunged, a burst of energy erupting from his palm aimed at Sage. With a swift, practiced motion, Sage deflected the attack, the spell dissipating harmlessly. Jim's eyes widened in surprise, but he recovered, hurling another volley of sinister magic.

Sage responded with a flurry of counterattacks, her paws a blur as bolts of light struck Jim with precision. She wasn't messing about. Each hit caused Jim to stagger, his confidence waning. He growled in frustration, his movements growing desperate.

"You think you can take me down, you little freak?" Jim spat, but his bravado was fading as he backed away.

Sage didn't bother to reply. She unleashed a wave of shimmering energy that sent Jim sprawling. He groaned, struggling to push himself up, but Sage was relentless. Another spell hit Jim square in the chest, knocking the wind out of him.

"I suggest you apologize to my friend and come to Angel Force to answer questions," I said.

Selena had kept a safe distance from the fight, but her hand was pressed against her chest and her eyes were wide with alarm. "Do it, babe. We have nothing to hide."

Jim glared up at Sage, hatred burning in his eyes, but he was too whipped to continue the fight. He collapsed back onto the ground, defeated. "Whatever. I ain't done nothing wrong, and I ain't got nothing to hide. And when that's proven, I'll expect a public apology and compensation."

"And I want a free-flowing salmon mousse fountain in my house, no gray in my fur, and hip joints that don't creak, but we don't get everything we want in life." Sage hissed at Jim until he got to his feet.

I was quick to restrain Jim just in case he got any dumb retaliation ideas, but this doped up irritation had no more fight left in him.

"You're not hurt, are you, baby-boo?" Selena hurried along beside Jim as he walked with his head down and his hands shackled behind his back, the crowd parting to let us through.

"It's only his pride that's been wounded and some light bruising," I said. "If he'd cooperated, none of this would have happened."

"You didn't have to be so rough with him," Selena said. "I need everything intact because I want at least six children."

Jim's head shot up. "Six kids! No, I've been there and done that. Having Azureus was enough."

"I doubt this man is capable of loving a child," I said to Selena. "Consider this a close call and find someone more acceptable."

She pouted. "I love this man, warts and all."

"Where exactly will we find these warts?" Sage asked.

"I ain't got no warts," Jim said. "There's nothing wrong with me. And there's no reason to take me in for questioning."

I looked over my shoulder. Reeny followed a short distance behind. I had a feeling he wouldn't run now Jim was going behind bars, but I was still undecided about Reeny. Someone in this party had committed this terrible crime, and I was determined to get to the bottom of it. Perhaps now we had them together, I could convince one of them to talk.

We arrived at Angel Force. I unlocked the door, and we went inside. After briefly checking on Adrienne and Joel, Selena, Jim, and Reeny got a cell each.

"Why are you locking me up? I've done nothing wrong other than stand by my man," Selena said.

"You need time to cool down," I said, "and think about your choice in men. Azureus was a much better boyfriend than Jim will ever be. You must have seen how badly Jim treated Azureus. You even told us when you came to Angel Force that Jim only ever used his son."

"He did it for the right reasons," Selena said. "Jim was much better at getting fungi out of Azureus than I was."

"So you were only in this weird love triangle to get your hands on more fungi?"

Selena flipped her hair over one shoulder. "A girl has needs. I stay with whoever can meet them best."

"You should have a serious conversation with yourself about where you want your future to unfurl. We'll be back to talk to you soon." I walked along the corridor with Sage, and we headed into the open-plan office and over to the murder board.

"I'm confused, hot, and hungry," Sage said. "Who knew solving a murder would be so complicated?"

"It's got me stumped, too. But before we talk murder, I have to say, you were amazing at the festival. Jim didn't stand a chance against you."

"That guy had it coming. It was nothing special. Let's focus on the suspects." Sage never enjoyed receiving a compliment.

I inspected the board. "All three of our suspects have a motive for wanting Azureus dead."

"Reeny wants out of his slave contract," Sage said. "Although I'm confused as to why he didn't flee Crimson Cove once he escaped Vorana's house. If he's guilty, it makes no sense he stuck around."

"He was determined to prove Jim guilty of murder," I said.

"Or frame him."

I nodded. "I no longer believe Reeny can't lie. He's been using that as a cover, so we didn't suspect him."

"Maybe he's said it to so many people so many times he convinced himself it was the truth," Sage said. "He's got to remain a suspect. Possibly the prime suspect."

I nodded. "And then we have Jim Stool. He has a perfect motive. It's clear he viciously resented Azureus's success. And now we discover Jim was carrying on with Selena behind his back."

"They could have fought. Azureus found out about the affair and confronted his dad. It got violent, and Jim strangled him."

"Jim has extra motives on extra motives," I said.

"But unfortunately, he has an alibi," Sage said.

"Selena. She does add a layer of complication," I murmured. "She only cares about what she can get out of Azureus's murder. But Selena was with Jim at Sorcha's café when Azureus was killed."

"Could they have snuck out of the café, gone back to the festival, and killed Azureus together?" Sage asked.

"There is a back way out of the café, but only the vampires use it," I said. "I doubt Sorcha would willingly let anyone creep out that way."

"They could have stumbled across the exit, made a plan, and headed back to the festival."

"Would Jim be so stupid as to take Florence on a date, having arranged to meet Selena so they could return to the festival and strangle Azureus? Jim must have realized Florence wouldn't wait all that time."

"He doesn't strike me as an over-thinker," Sage said. "He gets an idea, and even if it's wrong inside out and upside down, he'll go through with it. And maybe his experience with women has shown him they do wait. He's left ladies alone, come back for them, and they were still there, so he figured Florence would do the same."

"But Florence wasn't so gullible. She went looking for Jim and discovered him smooching Selena."

"Why make out in the bathroom when they should have been sneaking to the festival to murder Azureus?" Sage asked.

"Nervous excitement? And I've heard of curious types who get stimulated by the thought of murder." I stared at the murder board, wishing it would magically highlight the killer so we could end this mystery.

"That's gross. More like they were too full of their own self-importance and thought they'd have fun before going off to commit a heinous crime," Sage said. "The more time I spend with Jim and Selena, the lower my opinion of them becomes."

"I don't disagree. We've gotten everything we can out of Reeny for now," I said. "Let's speak to Jim. See if we can find a hole in his story."

We took a few moments to grab a snack and drinks from the kitchen then brought a cursing Jim into an interview room.

He slouched into a seat, scowling at us. "You can't get me for this murder. I'm innocent."

"We just want to ask a few questions," I said. "Let's start with your date with Florence."

He shrugged. "What about it?"

"Did you deliberately double-book two ladies for that night?" I asked.

A sharp smirk twisted his face. "It wouldn't be the first time. Sometimes, you take a lady out, and she's boring, or you get her under certain lighting, and you can see how old she is and how much makeup she's got caked on her face. I can't stand that. I like my women to be natural beauties. Got to keep my standards up."

"Obviously, being such a fine specimen yourself. So you arranged to take Florence on a date while also meeting Selena at the café in town?" I asked.

"Why not? They were both looking for fun, and so was I. It worked for all involved."

"Selena was happy about the plan?" Sage asked.

"I didn't care if she was happy or not. Despite what she tells you about all that marriage guff under a mushroom moon, we aren't serious. She gets weird ideas in her head and struggles to shake them loose. She'll move on soon enough and forget ever wanting to get hitched to me." Jim shuddered.

"The way she spoke, it sounds like you were the one who suggested marriage was on the cards," I said. "Did you mislead Selena to keep her around until you got her to do what you needed?"

"Needed? You've lost me." Jim picked dirt out from underneath a nail. "Despite what most women say, all they want is to be married. They feel like they have no role in life unless they've got a man to look after."

"Not the kind of women we know," I said.

Jim's smirk remained in place. "Selena is fun, but with Azureus dead, I realized she'd become a problem, and I wanted rid of her. I figured if she discovered me on a date with another woman, it would send her packing."

"You used Florence to annoy Selena?"

"Got it in one. I planned on enjoying myself with Florence at the festival, but we wouldn't have carried on after saying goodbye. Nobody would have been hurt, and we'd both have gotten what we wanted. The ladies love a piece of me," Jim said.

"You are an incredible catch," I replied.

Jim scowled at me. "Ask your questions so I can get out of here."

"You fooled around with Selena, but was that the only thing you did together?" I asked.

Jim tapped a finger on the table. "If I tell you everything, what do I get out of it?"

"That depends on how serious your crime is," I said. "If you murdered Azureus, there'll be little I can do to make your life easier. I may even delight in making it much harder."

"I didn't kill him. Azureus was my golden ticket. You don't tear that up. I may not be the smartest guy around here, but I'm no dummy."

"So what did you and Selena do together, apart from the obvious?"

"We'll talk about cutting a deal if I share?"

"I'll consider it," I said.

Jim grunted. "Selena was cute, and that cuteness helped with sales. I'd get fungi from Azureus then trade it on the black market for cheaper varieties. I'd get triple the amount of produce, and we'd cut the fungi with other herbs and dried bits of wood. That sort of thing. Once it was repackaged, we'd sell it. Selena was great at the sales. She'd flutter those big lashes, and the doped-up idiots would happily pay extra."

"Azureus found out what you were doing and confronted you?" I asked. "That's the reason you killed him?"

"Stop saying I killed my son! I used his reputation and our connection to inflate the prices. He never helped me. He got to the top and didn't reach down and lift me up to join him, so I had to figure things out for myself."

"What reason did you give him to help you?" I asked.

"I raised him. I'm owed. He was an annoying brat I had to put up with for years."

"A brat you should have supported, nurtured, and encouraged every step of the way when you saw his talent with fungi," I said. "Instead, you neglected him until he could give you something. Then you manipulated him."

"I'm his father! I got what I could out of him and then made deals with Selena. I kept her around because she made the selling and buying easier. She has a way of charming people. But I'm done with her if this marriage stuff gets serious. As soon as I can, I'm outta here."

"You won't be going anywhere if you're charged with murder," I said.

Jim leaned back. "If anyone wanted Azureus dead, it was Gilly."

"Gilly Piper? He has an alibi," I said.

"Maybe he does. Maybe he's a stinking liar. Now, I'm done talking. I want to see my lawyer," Jim said.

"We know you're involved." Sage jabbed a paw at Jim. "You're not getting away with this."

That slithering smirk reappeared. "I've got an alibi. She's sitting in your cell. Selena's with me, so you'll get nothing from her. This is a big waste of your time."

Unfortunately, I feared Jim was right.

But I wasn't giving up just yet.

Chapter 17

Secrets unfurl

"You always find it." Sage tossed a lump of raw steak at Joel. He jumped on it and devoured the meat, slurping and chomping noisily.

"Find what?" I was slumped beside her. Ever since the frustrating conversation with Jim, I'd lost my mojo. I couldn't figure out this problem. I refused to be defeated, but maybe I should change my thinking. Hang up the sleuthing cloak and admit defeat.

"The final clue." Sage hurled more steak, this time at Adrienne. "It's what you do. Everyone else is stuck, but you get to the truth."

"I only do that with Zandra. We figure these things out together."

"It's not like you to doubt yourself." Sage lobbed another chunk of steak, and Adrienne and Joel fought over it. "Behave! There's plenty to go around. We raided the top drawer of Vorana's freezer for you, so be grateful."

The ghouls growled their response and tore apart the steak.

"Without Zandra, I'm incomplete," I said.

"You sound like me," Sage said. "Do you want to find a roof to jump off? Or a toxic toadstool to chew on? We could go together. I want a last meal before we go, though. Not steak. Not after watching these two tear into the flesh. Maybe salmon. You love salmon."

"We're not jumping off roofs, eating dodgy mushrooms, or giving up," I said. "But I don't know what direction to take next. We've questioned the suspects, and uncovered numerous motives, but we're no closer to working out which one did it."

"We could focus on the giving up option." Sage tossed the last piece of steak into the cell for the ghouls to fight over. "These two have. They've gone feral. When the angels come to their senses, Adrienne and Joel are done for."

"They've been affected by whatever's polluting Crimson Cove," I said. "Adrienne and Joel will be fine."

"And we come back to that old problem," Sage said. "What is polluting our town? Why is everyone else being weird, but we're not?"

"Because we're special," I said.

"Speak for yourself. I'm as unremarkable as they come."

"Untrue, and you know it. Your fight with Jim and your pursuit of Reeny were extraordinary. You pull the weak, old cat act to get sympathy from Vorana, but you don't need to. She adores you just as you are."

"I like being a weak, old cat. It means I get carried around and extra treats. And Vorana cuts up all my food, so I barely need to chew. It's comforting."

"It's lazy! There's no need to be slow and greedy to get what you want," I said.

Sage stared at the ghouls. "Is that why Vorana left? She got bored with my grumpy old cat attitude?"

"Whether you were a young cat full of beans and bouncing around, or the stinky old creature you currently inhabit, it wouldn't matter to her. You're bonded, so you're together for life."

"We may be bonded, but just like you, I feel abandoned," Sage said. "We can't go on like this. Our days can't be this meaningless."

"Solving a murder and keeping Adrienne and Joel safe from harm is hardly pointless."

"So solve it!" Sage said. "Find the final clue and get this over with. Perhaps when Crimson Cove isn't being so bizarre, Zandra and Vorana will come home."

I hoped that was true. The unsettled atmosphere in Crimson Cove had stirred things to an uncomfortable level of uncertainty. There had to be a reason why Zandra left, and it couldn't be me.

"We have the lying dad, the cheating girlfriend, or the nervy slave elf," Sage said. "Let's charge them all."

"I'm interested in Gilly," I said.

"Jim only brought his name up to take the heat off himself. Gilly's got an alibi."

"Perhaps. Before we find Gilly, let's speak to our lying elf," I said. "Reeny must have seen a few things while serving Azureus and Jim. Perhaps he knows why Jim pointed the finger at Gilly."

"We can't trust anything that comes out of that little jerk's mouth," Sage said. "It could all be lies. He could be the killer!"

"He could. But I want to dig more. Adrienne and Joel will quiet down now they've been fed, so they won't make so much noise. We'll get Reeny out and chat with him. Keep it friendly so as not to startle him into quivering silence."

"Or we could threaten to feed him to the ghouls. That'll get the irritating punk talking."

"Let's keep that as Option B."

Five minutes later, we were in an interview room with a nervous Reeny shifting in his seat, refusing to meet our gaze.

"Have you charged Jim yet?" he finally asked.

"Jim is refusing to confess, and we've not got enough evidence to charge him with murder," I said. "But we're interested in your thoughts about Gilly Piper. Jim suggested we look at him as the killer."

"Gilly! Well, I suppose it's possible, given everything that happened. I still think it was Jim."

"What happened?" Sage asked.

Reeny sniffed. "The broken engagement. But I think he's over that."

"Who was engaged to whom?" I asked.

"Gilly was engaged to Azureus's aunt. An auntie from his father's side. Her name was Tabitha. They met through Azureus. Aunt Tabitha went to an event he was speaking at and got introduced to Gilly. They hit it off and started dating."

"They got engaged, but something went wrong?" I asked.

"Azureus didn't approve of the engagement," Reeny said. "He was fine if they kept things casual, but when Gilly announced they planned to marry, he was furious. He didn't do anything at first, but I watched him, and I could tell he was plotting."

"He forced his aunt to break off the engagement?"

"I don't have all the facts, but I heard a few things." Reeny squirmed in his seat.

"Azureus is dead, so you're not betraying him by telling us what happened," I said. "And you could provide us with the vital clue we need to figure out who actually killed him."

Reeny shuffled about some more. "I sometimes listen at keyholes. Azureus would have private meetings that even I was excluded from. One day, he invited Aunt Tabitha over for coffee. He made her an offer she couldn't refuse. On one condition."

"She broke the engagement with Gilly," I said.

Reeny nodded. "Aunt Tabitha always wanted a vineyard. She had a passion for wine and longed to have a place of her own. The problem was, she had little magic. Nothing of value developed, and many people didn't consider her part of the magic community. She was an outcast. That meant she only ever had low-paid jobs and struggled to get by."

"But Azureus came along and offered her something she'd always dreamed of," I said. "Do you think she loved Gilly?"

"There was a fondness there. But Gilly adored Tabitha. He cared nothing about her lowly status or her lack of useful magic. He just wanted her."

"And Tabitha was happy to marry up?"

"She liked Gilly. He's smart, maybe a bit self-important, but he's not a cruel man. I'd have no objections if he was my master," Reeny said. "I imagine Aunt Tabitha saw a comfortable life ahead of her by marrying Gilly."

"But it couldn't have been true love for her if she abandoned Gilly so easily," I said.

"Azureus knew her weakness. They'd often talk about her dream of owning a vineyard and having land and a small place to live. He paid for it all and even became an investor in the vineyard to ensure its success," Reeny said.

"You heard all that through a keyhole?" Sage asked.

Reeny blushed. "I may have seen a few relevant documents when cleaning Azureus's office."

"Azureus brought into the vineyard to ensure it wouldn't fail, thus keeping Tabitha from returning to Gilly," I said.

"It gives Gilly a great motive for killing Azureus," Sage said. "He must have found out what Azureus did and taught him a lesson."

"If he did figure out the reason the relationship ended, I don't know how he managed it," Reeny said. "Part of the deal with Aunt Tabitha was that she could never tell anyone Azureus bought her the vineyard and invested in her business. She signed a contract that said, if she told anybody, she'd have to give it all back. She had no problem with that and happily signed the deal."

"You knew about it," I said. "Did you tell Gilly?"

"Absolutely not! I'm appalled you'd even think that," Reeny said. "Azureus wasn't always easy to work for, but I was loyal to him. I never shared his secrets."

"Because he ordered you not to, but now he's dead, you can say whatever you like about him," I said.

"Well, that's true. But I wouldn't have been able to tell anyone about the deal he made with Aunt Tabitha while he was alive," Reeny said. "Gilly didn't hear the news from me. And there was no happy ending for Aunt Tabitha. She died at the vineyard. Crushed by a barrel."

"Maybe Gilly learned of her death and put the pieces together," I said. "Filled with rage and revenge, he plotted Azureus's downfall."

"The problem with Gilly as the murderer is he has a good alibi," Sage said. "He was with Kinoko, munching their way through enchanted mushrooms as part of their weird meditation."

"Oh, that," Reeny said. "You know what kind of meditation they do, don't you?"

"Kinoko mentioned some kind of interdimensional work," I said.

"It's more than that. They go full-on out-of-body experience," Reeny said. "When they're in that zone, it's impossible to reach them. Azureus took part in one of their sessions, and I thought he'd died. They sit still or lie on the ground, barely breathing as they float away."

"They must get disturbed by noise or people coming into the room," I said.

"Nothing gets them out of their meditative state until they're ready to return," Reeny said.

"Which means, if Gilly is our killer, he could have faked his meditation and, once Kinoko was under, snuck off and strangled Azureus," I said. "Then he returned and pretended he'd been there the whole time. Kinoko would have been none the wiser."

"Maybe Jim shared Tabitha's secret," Sage said. "He knew how angry Gilly would be. He wanted Azureus dead so he could get his grasping, mushroom-addled hands on the money and fungi."

"I wish that were true, but Jim had no clue about the deal made between Aunt Tabitha and Azureus," Reeny said. "They knew what he was like and trusted him with nothing."

"We must speak to Gilly," I said. "This gives him a much clearer motive for wanting Azureus dead. Azureus took away the love of his life, and then she died. Even if Gilly didn't know for certain Azureus had a hand in spoiling things with Aunt Tabitha, he could have guessed something happened. After all, Tabitha was poor and had no status, and suddenly she gets this massive vineyard and a house of her own."

"Gilly asked lots of questions when she left him. He even asked me if I knew what was going on, but of course, I was loyal to Azureus," Reeny said. "Aunt Tabitha explained it away by saying she'd come into an inheritance from a dead relative. Gilly pressed for details, but she said she didn't want to talk about it."

"More likely, she didn't want to make a mistake and lose everything," I said.

There was a brief silence as I considered this information. Had Jim been useful for once by pointing at Gilly? Or was Reeny right, and this was a ruse to buy him time until his lawyer arrived to tie us up in red tape in the hope of getting out on a technicality?

"May I leave now?" Reeny asked. "I've given you as much information as I can."

"Not yet," I said. "We're keeping you, Jim, and Selena here until we learn the truth."

"But those ghouls are terrifying," Reeny said. "And they can smell me. They want to eat me."

"That doesn't make you special," Sage said. "They want to eat all of us."

"It won't be for much longer," I said to Reeny. "You'll soon be free."

"Providing we don't find evidence that proves you're the killer," Sage said.

Reeny sighed. "Free. You mean, I get to return to a life of slavery with Jim?"

"It's no less than you deserve," Sage said. "Even now, you're hiding and concealing things. You should have told us about the vineyard deal upfront."

"I didn't think it was relevant!" Reeny said. "And I'm still convinced Jim is the killer. Please, don't abandon me. I know I've done wrong by you, but I want to make amends. I'm an excellent cook. I could visit every morning for the next year and make you breakfast."

"One drugged breakfast from you was quite enough to last a lifetime," I said.

Reeny's bottom lip trembled, but he nodded.

Once Reeny was back in his cell, we left Angel Force and returned to the festival to find Gilly. We hadn't even reached the main entrance before it became clear things were out of control. Two giant trash cans were ablaze, a group of people were embroiled in a vicious-looking fight, and the stalls looked like they'd been cleaned out of all stock and then demolished.

"What in the heck has gone on here?" Sage asked.

Cythera appeared and danced with a group of her angels in a conga line, hitting people with their wings as they frolicked and laughed.

"The place is being destroyed. And our town will be next." I was almost knocked off my paws as Sammy bounded past with Binky and Archie.

"Sammy! What are you doing?" I yelled.

Sammy slowed as he glanced over his shoulder. "Getting as far away from you as possible. You stink."

I blinked at him in surprise. "You've been affected, too?"

"Ignore her," Archie said. "She's too much of a freak to hang around with. Let's go set something on fire."

"Don't listen to them." Sage gently nudged me with her shoulder. "They're as messed up as everybody else. Sammy adores you."

It was hard not to listen, though. Sammy had been a steadfast companion for a long time. I couldn't lose him, too.

"Hey, stop frowning. Don't we have a murder to solve?" Sage asked. "Once we're done with that, we'll deal with these idiots."

I watched as Sammy, Binky, and Archie bounced off together. How quickly my happy little world had fallen apart. Nothing felt secure.

I yelped as something stung my butt. Sage had whacked me with a clawed murder mitten. "Why did you do that?"

"I see Gilly!" Sage said. "He just collapsed behind a marquee."

I forced my thoughts away from Sammy and followed Sage to the marquee, dodging the chaos and mess. Gilly was sprawled on his back, laughing at the sky.

I jumped onto his chest and glared down at him. "We need to talk about your broken engagement with Tabitha."

Chapter 18

Sage succumbs

"My broken engagement?" Gilly roared with laughter, enveloping me in his stale, moldy breath. "Why do you care about that?"

"Because it gives you a motive for murdering Azureus," I said.

"Oh! Well, I suppose it does. I thought you were asking because you were interested in dating me. I've never dated fluffy, but I'm open-minded." Gilly chuckled to himself.

"You were engaged to Azureus's Aunt Tabitha, weren't you?" I said. "And she ditched you."

The laughter faded, and Gilly fished in his jacket pocket, pulled out a handful of dried mushrooms, and shoved them into his mouth. "What of it?"

"She broke off the engagement after coming into some money. That must have made you angry," I said. "She no longer needed you to provide for her, so you got dumped."

"That had nothing to do with it. And unless you want to set me up with someone, my failed relationships have nothing to do with you. Have some dried fungi. I raided one of the last stalls still standing. It's good stuff."

"It makes you lose your mind and roll about in the dirt, laughing at nothing," Sage said.

I batted away Gilly's hand. "Keep that stuff away from me. It's trouble."

"There's nothing troubling about nature," Gilly said. "That's what I love about fungi. All natural ingredients. Nothing artificial. Nothing nasty."

"There are plenty of things in nature that will kill you," Sage said. "And I include us in that."

Gilly stared at Sage and then burst into another bout of laughter, displaying the chewed-up fungi.

I batted Gilly on the cheek several times to get his attention. Claws were extended. "Azureus was murdered by someone at this festival. You've been honest about how much you disliked him and how unfair you thought it was that he got his position even though he had no training. Now we've uncovered information that Azureus's aunt broke off her engagement with you."

"I don't see the relevance. Are you sure you don't want any fungi? Tastes like orange chocolate." He attempted to shove a piece into my mouth, but I whacked it away, and it bounced into the dirt.

"Do you know why Tabitha broke off the engagement?" Sage asked.

Gilly reached for the dirt encrusted fungi. "She told me she needed to focus on her business. I said I'd be happy to wait for her, but her vineyard was a long way away, so..."

"It didn't bother you that the engagement ended?" I asked. "From what I've learned, you loved

Tabitha, so you must have been devastated when you found out she'd died."

The glazed look in Gilly's eyes vanished for a few seconds. "Yeah. She was special. She even enjoyed listening to me talk about my forest finds. Tabitha liked to see me happy. She had a generous heart. I was sorry I couldn't capture it. Can you grab that fungi for me?"

"No. It's filthy. Tabitha liked you, but she wanted her vineyard more," I said.

"You've lost me on that comment." Gilly finally got the fungi, blew the dirt off, and ate it. "She could have had us both. I even said I'd move to be closer, but she wasn't interested. The grapes came first."

"And that didn't make you suspicious?"

"Of what?"

I glanced at Sage, and she nodded. It was time to reveal all. "You must have known what Azureus did for her."

"Err... They were related, so I'm assuming he helped her out now and again. What are you getting at?"

"There was no inheritance," Sage said. "And we think you found out exactly how Tabitha got her dream vineyard. We've been told you were asking questions about where she got all of her money after she left you."

Gilly remained flat on his back, staring at the sky. "It was strange. But these things happen. You read about it sometimes, some old relative you've never met and only heard about in passing, leaving everything to you. It was like something out of a story."

"That's because it wasn't true," I said. "Who told you it was Azureus who gave Tabitha the vineyard?"

"I... I don't know. I don't remember. Help me up, and we can search the stalls. There could be more fungi hidden away."

"Forget the disgusting fungi and focus on the conversation," Sage said. "Who told you about Azureus helping his aunt?"

Gilly sighed.

"You did know?" I asked.

There was more sighing. "Of course. And no one told me. A while back, I decided to surprise Tabitha and took a trip to her vineyard. I wanted to convince her we could make it work. Long-distance relationships are tough, but I loved her. When I arrived, Azureus was there, so I hung back and waited for him to leave. I didn't like the guy and didn't want to spend any time with him."

I flicked an ear. "So you listened to their private conversation?"

"Why not? It wouldn't have been a problem if they didn't keep secrets," Gilly said. "They were standing outside her house talking, and she thanked him for everything. Azureus pretended to know nothing and said it was their secret. He made her promise not to tell. That's when I figured it out."

"You knew Azureus didn't want you marrying his aunt?" I asked.

"The guy never wanted me happy. I don't know what I did to offend him, but he had it in for me. He took all the best jobs, got the promotion meant for me, and then took Tabitha away from me. Then she died."

"Since we've been investigating this murder, you've said plenty of unkind things about Azureus," I said. "It's no surprise he was hesitant about letting you become a part of his family."

"If I'd joined the family, I'd have supported him more," Gilly said. "I hated his arrogance and his know-it-all approach about fungi, but I'd have died for Tabitha. I really loved her."

"And when you learned she abandoned you because of what Azureus had done, you must have been blind with rage. Furious enough to attack Azureus," I said.

Gilly checked his pockets and came up empty. He grimaced. "I didn't kill Azureus. Let's go look for fungi. I need more. I can't get enough of the stuff."

"You've had plenty," I said. "Admit you killed Azureus. You pretended to meditate with Kinoko then snuck off and caught Azureus unawares. You needed to be stealthy, so rather than blasting him with magic and risk him fighting back, you strangled him. What did you use?"

"Nothing! Because that didn't happen," Gilly said. "I understand why you think I'm involved, but I'm too interested in my career to ruin everything by killing Azureus. And if I hated the guy that much, I wouldn't shout about it and tell you how much I disliked the smug moron. I'd keep it to myself while I made plans to get rid of him."

"Some people have an inability to keep their mouths shut," Sage said. "They open their chops, and all the blah, blah, blah falls out."

"Not me. I've gotten rid of business rivals before, and no one raised an eyebrow," Gilly said.

"Not by murdering them, though. Or have you?" I asked.

Gilly rolled his eyes. "I'm glad Tabitha refused to marry me. It meant I didn't have to fake being nice to Azureus. I'd have done it for her, but it would have been hard." He shoved his hands into his jacket pockets. "Hey, I found another couple of bits. One for me, and one for you." He pushed a piece of dried truffle into Sage's mouth.

"Spit that out!" I said to her. "You don't know where it's been or what it'll do to you."

"Too late. I swallowed it," Sage said. "I didn't mean to, but it was instinct. Will it kill me?"

Gilly laughed. "It's just fungi!"

I whacked him with a murder mitten. "What was in that fungi? What will it do to my friend?"

"Relax her. And you need some, too."

"I need nothing that'll impair my judgment," I said. "Until we sort out this mess, you're joining the rest of the suspects at Angel Force."

"Who else are you trying to frame for this murder?" Gilly asked. "Surely, you only need one of us, and then you can close this case and let your fur down. Ha! Let your fur down. That was good."

"I don't want any of you escaping," I said. "You're all acting strangely, so I don't know what you'll do next. Make a bonfire of our town, if we're not careful."

Gilly chuckled. "How about this for an amazing plan? You help me search the rest of the stalls for goodies, and I'll come willingly to Angel Force. You can lock me in a cell if you like, so long as I have my fungi with me. I've got nothing to hide."

"Not anymore you don't," I said. "Not since we uncovered your secret about Tabitha."

"I'm hardly going to brag about being dumped by the woman I loved," Gilly said. "Do we have a deal? But I need all hands on deck to hunt the treats. Although that should be paws. I have hands, you understand." He jazz-handed us, which made him laugh again.

I was done being nice to this guy. I knocked Gilly back with a spell and turned to Sage. She wobbled on her front paws and was drooling.

"Are you unwell? It must be the fungi. Stick your paw down your throat to make yourself sick." I hopped over to my friend.

"No! I feel groovy. I like these mushrooms. We should have tried them earlier. Why did we hold out for so long?"

My heart sank to my toe beans. "Not you, too. Sage, I need you. I can't do this alone. Zandra's gone. My magical misfits have disbanded, and everything is turned upside down. Stay with me, old friend. Fight this. Don't abandon me."

"Fight what? We should help Gilly search for fungi."

"Gilly is going into a cell until we can figure out if he's a killer," I said. "Sage! Focus! Don't give in."

"Fungi first, fungi first," Gilly chanted, and Sage joined in, wobbling over to where he was sprawled.

I stepped away as they chaotically jigged about. Was the whole town about to be lost? And if it was, should I care? All my friends had changed, and Zandra had left me. With everything ripped apart beyond repair and what I thought would be my forever home in chaos, it could be time to make a change. I should abandon Crimson Cove and start again.

There were ways to break a bond with a magic user if things went wrong. I could go back to being solo. I'd managed before. But it hadn't been a fun life, more of a miserable existence. Could I do that again? Give up everything I held so dear?

I looked at the fires blazing, the angels misbehaving, and Sage floating in the air next to Gilly while they chanted about fungi. I hated the idea of abandoning Crimson Cove, but if there was nothing left to save, was it my time to go?

"Let's go fungi hunting," Sage said. "Forget the murder. It's boring."

"I'm sorry, you won't like me for doing this," I said.

"Doing what?" Sage grunted as I blasted her with a knockout spell, and she hit the dirt. I did the same to Gilly, although he resisted, and I had to whack him hard several times before he finally succumbed.

I conjured a spell to float them safely back to Angel Force and away from the chaos. It was quickly spreading, and there were revelers misbehaving along the main street in Crimson Cove. Several storefronts had been broken into and were being raided. There was also an odd haze of magic in the air, and there was a smell of rot I couldn't get out of my booping snooter. The town and its people were decaying in front of my eyes.

I slowed as I got close to Voss's pizza parlor. The place was full of a rowdy crowd, who were eating and fighting at the same time. Remus was there with his vampires around him. They were randomly grabbing passersby and feeding on them.

I took a step forward, meaning to stop them, but I was outnumbered. If Remus set his vampire hive on me, I'd be nothing more than a husk, and I'd lose the opportunity to unpick this terrible problem.

I was almost knocked over by a crowd of people rushing past, hooting and wailing as they shoved their way into the pizza parlor. It seemed this was the new place to be if you wanted to add mayhem and chaos to your life.

Roland and Nimbus passed me, looking surprisingly happy despite the bedlam.

"Roland! The festival is out of control," I said. "What happened?"

He slowed and turned, one hand settling on Nimbus. "It is chaotic, isn't it?"

"That's an understatement. It's time to shut the festival. Send everyone home before things get worse."

"Leave, you should," Nimbus said. "Not welcome here you are."

"This is my home. I'm staying right here."

"Find your missing witch, you should. Focus on that, not this."

"I can focus on more than one thing at a time," I said.

"What are you doing with Gilly?" Roland asked. "Is he injured?"

"He's a suspect in Azureus's murder," I said. "I'm taking him in for questioning."

"Oh! Of course. I've been so busy with the festival that I forgot," Roland said.

"You forgot about stumbling over a body and passing out in shock?" I asked.

Roland looked momentarily perplexed. "I must have done. How strange. And I even forgot to write it in my notepad. I put everything in there. It's important to remember everybody's movements. I could miss something important if I don't write it down. The old memory is not what it used to be."

"I don't suppose you wrote down anything useful after finding Azureus's body, did you?" I asked.

"Wasting time, we are," Nimbus said. "Must join the party."

"Sorry, Juno. We're having a feast at the pizza parlor. You can come, although it looks like you've got your hands full." Roland gestured at Gilly and Sage.

"Not welcome, she is," Nimbus said. "Nosy troublemaker."

Nimbus had always been mean, so I expected those kinds of comments from her. "Be careful if you're going to the pizza parlor. It's rowdy. And the vampires are biting people."

"I bite back," Nimbus said. "Regret it if they bite us."

"Nimbus always protects me," Roland said. "I'd be nothing without her. I hope you solve the murder. And I'm glad it didn't ruin the festival for everybody else."

"No, the fires, looting, and random fighting did that. You must see how wrong this is."

"Party we must go to," Nimbus said. "Ignore. Ignore. No one likes Juno."

"Hey! Even for you, that's nasty," I said.

"Yes, the party is the most important thing." Roland turned and scurried away, while Nimbus looked over her shoulder and snarled at me. Spiteful creature.

I turned toward Angel Force and then stopped. The pizza parlor. Everything went wrong after Roland and Voss mixed up the enchanted truffles in the food served to Remus and his vampires. That mix-up led to Altruist's girlfriend staking him on a tree. We'd never fully solved how the mix-up happened, and Roland and Voss swore every which way that they hadn't made a mistake. They were professionals and genuinely nice people, so it was put down to an innocent accident.

I looked at Vorana's bookstore, which fortunately hadn't been ravaged, although had yet to be repaired after a cauldron containing a boiled magic user was tipped over and soaked the floor. That was the scene of Nahla's murder. She'd been killed by her husband, Ivan, after he'd discovered she'd been drugging him for years to keep him subservient.

Petra's death had followed shortly afterward and had never been fully explained. Ivan wasn't convinced he'd done it, but he'd been such a confused mess that he'd confessed to the crime. But the way Petra had been murdered was vicious, and just like Azureus, there'd been thin red marks on her skin.

Was that a coincidence?

I didn't believe in such a thing. There was something much bigger and darker behind this. But who was causing it, and why?

As I hurried toward Angel Force, floating Sage and an unconscious Gilly beside me, I knew I couldn't give up on Crimson Cove until I found out the truth.

Chapter 19

Final clue

I rolled over and stared at the empty space beside me on Zandra's bed. I'd never get used to this. Those brief thoughts about abandoning Crimson Cove, breaking my bond with Zandra, and starting afresh were wrong.

This was my home, and my family was here. Every single messed-up one of them. From the curmudgeonly Sage, who was now locked in a cell for her own protection, to the flamboyant, over-the-top Remus, who hosted elaborate parties and did his best not to break the rules, although he frequently failed. They were my family, and they needed help.

I shook out my glorious fur and hopped off the bed. It was my responsibility to fix this mess. I hadn't caused it, but I'd get to the bottom of who had. Although I'd do it alone, and that was my least favorite way to work. I didn't blame Sage for abandoning me at a crucial moment in this investigation. I knew what the problem was. After seeing Sage change when she'd been force-fed that strange truffle by Gilly, this murky mess boiled down to one thing. Fungi.

Everything that was wrong in Crimson Cove came back to mushrooms. The mistakes made at Voss's pizza parlor, everyone's behavior changing when the tea shop opened and Nahla Gerbolt showed up with her enchanted tea blends laced with mushrooms, and finally the enormous fungi festival. The town had been slowly drugged by treats, and no one realized it until it was too late for them to do anything about it.

"Well, I know," I said to myself. "And now I have the source of the problem, I'm going straight to it. After I've eaten." I recognized the value of sleep and nourishment to ensure I was on top form to bring down a powerful enemy.

I headed up the basement steps and spent a few moments rifling around in Vorana's pantry. There was barely anything left. Sage and I hadn't been restrictive with our rations. But I found an out-of-date bag of dried beef jerky tucked at the back, and after shredding it open with my claws, I tucked in.

Now, it was down to business. All this weird fungi nonsense had started with Roland Moldsworth. He'd arrived in town obsessing over fungi and excited to spread the mushroomy love, and everything had tipped upside down. I always knew to watch the quiet ones, but Roland had been so skittish and shy, I'd overlooked him. That was my mistake. A mistake I planned on rectifying.

It was early as I left the house. No one else was around, but the evening's previous excesses were clear to see. Most of the stores had been looted, and I had to pause and put out a few small fires still burning in trash cans.

When the residents came back to their senses, we'd need to pull together to make everything right.

And I had hope. When Crimson Cove worked, it really worked. And as I was discovering, when it didn't, it was a giant fireball of terrifying ickiness. But that's what happened when a bunch of immensely powerful magic users in a bad mood were under the influence of something tainted and toxic.

As I walked to Roland's house, I thought about how I wanted this to go. Roland was a timid little thing, but Nimbus was no slouch. And she'd defend Roland if I came after him hard. I needed to reason with him. Lay out the evidence and ask him to surrender. If he refused, then things would get serious. Obliteration level serious.

And a part of me desired that obliteration. Roland's devious behavior meant I'd lost Zandra. But now I knew the source of the trouble, I could defeat it and get her back.

Buoyed with determination, I hurried along the street to Roland's home. I peered through a window into his front room. Roland was sprawled out asleep in a chair, and surprisingly, there was no sign of Nimbus. They were always together.

I looked in a few other windows, but Nimbus was nowhere to be seen. I assumed she must be eating breakfast or in the backyard. But other than the occasional white tuft of her fur drifting in the air currents, she was missing.

I completed a circuit of the house then tested the front door. As I'd expected, it was locked. Roland was judicious. I couldn't imagine him falling asleep and leaving himself unprotected, especially when he had so many secrets to conceal.

I returned to the backyard and looked for a way in. As I was searching, a scratching sound reached me. I looked around the yard, but there was no sign of any burrowing animals. The sound came from the garden shed.

Cautiously, I approached, ready to spring into action if some crazed fungi-doped creature burst out. I cracked the door open an inch, and my eyes widened. Nimbus was shackled inside, a thick loop of chain wrapped around her body.

I opened the door wider and hurried in. "What happened to you?"

Nimbus hissed at me and flared her fur.

I hissed back. "I'm not here to harm you. Who chained you in this shed?"

After more hissing and growling, Nimbus quietened. "Roland."

"Why would your bonded magic user chain you up?"

"I love him. Loyal to him, I am."

"We're all loyal to those we're bonded with, but if Roland is hurting you, you can't stay with him," I said. "Has he done this before?"

"Tried to help him, I have. He can't be stopped."

I sighed. "I know Roland is behind the problems in Crimson Cove. Do you also know what he's been doing?"

She nodded, her long furry body quivering. "First, fun it was. But he's gone insane. He tried to kill me last night when we came home. I begged him not to, so he tossed me in here and wrapped me in chains."

"Let me get you free. I'm so sorry this happened." I crept closer, aware that Nimbus had long, sharp teeth and was keen on using them.

"He was angry yesterday when I told him no more. He's had too many fungi. It's infected him with something dark." Nimbus rippled and writhed as I got within touching distance.

I tugged gently at the chains. They were wrapped tightly around Nimbus, and I didn't want to hurt her. "Has Roland got some grand plan?"

"Just an addled brain, he has. He longs for chaos. He thinks this is fun."

"Are you helping him grow that chaos?"

She grumbled to herself. "At first. Not now. Too dangerous. Bad I feel for the betrayal."

"Don't feel bad. Everyone is behaving out of character. Zandra left to look for a new adventure, and she took Vorana with her. They'd never abandon Sage and me if they were thinking straight." I succeeded in un-looping a piece of chain. I checked Nimbus wasn't about to pounce, but she stayed low on the shed floor. "And everyone at the mushroom festival has lost control. Did Roland set up the festival to gather an army of chaos makers?"

"Share his plans with me, he doesn't. Not anymore. Scared of him, I am."

"That must be tough," I said. "You should never be afraid of the magic user you've bonded with. Don't bite me, but I need to tug hard on this chain to get it loose, or you won't be able to get out."

Nimbus growled menacingly but made no move to attack as I finally got the chain loose enough for her to slide free.

Just as Nimbus got out, Roland shoved open the door to the yard and stumbled outside. He looked at us, his eyes bleary and confusion filling his face. "No! What are you—"

"Stop him, we must." Nimbus blasted Roland in the chest with a spell. He staggered back, hitting the house, his eyes wide with shock, his hands raised, a spell growing.

"Dangerous magic. Must be defeated." Nimbus swiped me with a tail I'd never seen before. "Help?"

Adrenaline surged through me as Roland righted himself and swirled a weak spell into being.

"Please, there's been a mistake," he implored.

Nimbus and I shared a quick glance, and I nodded, knowing we had to act fast.

Nimbus darted forward, her fur bristling with energy. She sent another bolt of magic toward Roland, but he deflected it with a clumsy shield. The spell ricocheted off and shattered a garden ornament.

I circled to the left, my magic crackling in the air. I needed to distract Roland to give Nimbus an opening. I conjured a whirlwind of leaves and debris, sending it spiraling.

Roland flinched and stumbled, trying to maintain his focus on the spell he cast, his words lost in the whirlwind of debris. His spell fizzled and popped, sending harmless sparks into the air. Roland's face twisted in frustration as he tried again, but Nimbus leaped into the air, claws extended, and raked at his protective shield, her magic flaring bright and fierce.

I launched a binding spell, thick tendrils of energy snaking toward Roland. He barely managed to sidestep, but the effort cost him, and he broke through his own protective magic. Nimbus pounced again, her teeth bared, and swiped at his arm, leaving a deep cut.

Roland yelped, his concentration breaking. His magic faltered, and Nimbus took advantage, hitting him with a stun spell. He staggered back again, eyes wide with fear and pain.

I summoned a burst of light, blinding him temporarily, and Nimbus followed with a powerful blast that sent Roland crashing to the ground. For someone with so much powerful chaos magic, he was barely able to defend himself. It must be the effects of all that fungi.

Roland tried to crawl away, but I was on him in an instant, pinning him with a spell.

Nimbus stood over him, panting heavily, her eyes blazing with fury. Roland lay there, helpless and defeated, his eyes pleading.

I didn't feel pity. He'd caused too much harm, hurt too many people. I tightened the magical bonds, ensuring he couldn't escape. "I know you're behind this mess. And anyone who harms their familiar is a monster."

"Beyond saving, some may say. Destroy him we should," Nimbus said.

I peered at her. I'd never consider destroying Zandra, no matter how twisted or bitter she became. Roland must have grievously injured Nimbus for her to consider ending him. "Roland must pay for his crimes. People have died because of his actions, and everyone has been adversely affected by him slipping tainted fungi into our food and drink."

"I'd never do that!" Roland quivered beneath my paws. "I love this town. And I love my fungi. It helps, not harms."

"You love fungi too much," I said. "You've grown greedy with the power it has given you. It's corrupted your mind. You need a long spell of rehab, but then you must answer for your crimes."

"Please, you must believe me. I like a quiet life. My simple hobbies. Why would I want to turn Crimson Cove chaotic? It doesn't serve me."

"Talking nonsense, he is," Nimbus said. "Bad man. Ashamed of you, I am."

Roland thumped his fists into the dirt. "Why won't anyone believe me?"

"Because the evidence reveals your guilt," I said. "I should have remained suspicious when the problems began at Voss's pizza parlor. But you were so helpful and sincere. You convinced me you had nothing to do with Altruist being staked by his girlfriend, or Remus growing cold and suspicious of his friends."

"I didn't do that! Neither did Voss."

"You murdered Petra, didn't you?" I asked. "When I discovered her on the beach, there were red whip-like marks on her skin. I assumed it was due to seaweed binding around her flesh, but whatever murder weapon was used on her left those marks. What was it?"

Roland blinked rapidly. "Nothing! Because I didn't do it."

"Did Petra discover what you were up to?" I asked. "She was no fool. She must have seen you do something shady and threatened to expose you to Angel Force, so you silenced her."

"I don't know what you're talking about," Roland said. "Of course, I heard about her murder, but I'm not behind it. Why would I want a stranger dead?"

"Perhaps she read your tea leaves and saw your dark heart," I said. "Nimbus, did you and Roland have your tea leaves read recently?"

"We did," Nimbus said. "Roland was scared."

Roland's panicked, fear-filled gaze flashed to Nimbus. "Why are you lying? I've always looked after you."

"I found Nimbus chained in a shed!" I said. "That's cruelty, not kindness."

"I didn't do that to her." Roland sniffed back tears. "I'm begging you, let me go. I'll tell you everything."

"We already know the truth," I said. "You're coming with me. You'll show me how to reverse the problems caused by your tainted fungi, and then we're fixing this town. After that, you're going behind bars for a very long time."

Roland grabbed at me, but before his fingers wrapped around my middle, Nimbus lashed out with a long thin tongue and bound his wrists with it. She jumped forward, dragged Roland through the dirt, causing him to yelp and me to leap to safety. She stood over him, about to bite.

"Nimbus! No! Let go of Roland," I said. "If he's dead, he can't be punished."

"Evil man," Nimbus said. "Must be silenced for good."

I whacked her hard with a spell and sent her flying. Her tongue unfurled from around Roland's wrists, leaving behind thin red whip-like marks.

I sucked in a breath as Nimbus rolled to her belly and hissed at me.

"My right. Terrible man. Hurt me. Hurt your town. We destroy him together."

"It was you." I shook with shock. "You're the villain behind all of this."

Nimbus's fur fluffed. "No! Him! Roland is evil."

I inspected Roland's wrists. They were the same marks as those found on Petra's body and identical to the strangulation mark on Azureus's neck. "It all makes sense. You and Roland are always together, so it would have been simple for you to mix up the herbs on the pizzas to send the vampires feral. And you killed Petra because she caught you doing something you shouldn't. What did she see you do?"

Nimbus simply hissed at me, growing bigger by the second as her fur fluffed.

"The same goes for Azureus," I continued. "Did he see you tampering with the produce at the festival? Casting spells over batches of fungi to turn people crazy? Or had he always been suspicious of you? Roland is deeply involved in the fungi community, which meant Azureus could have seen something troubling when you attended an event.

Or perhaps his natural talent for identifying rare and powerful fungi alerted him that you were mixing damaging fungi into food."

A low rumbling laugh drifted out of Nimbus. "Juno, always so naïve, you are. I shouldn't be surprised you didn't recognize me. Ever since I've known you, you've been so full of your own self-importance."

I reared back, another quiver of shock hitting me. "We know each other? How?"

"We've been enemies for a long time. But hidden in this form, you had no idea of the problems I would bring down on your head."

"This form? What are you?" My heart beat fast as I attempted to see through Nimbus's disguise.

"Let me give you a brief reminder of my magnificence." Nimbus leapt into the air, sparks of magic flying off her. Several pinged into me, and I got a taste of how powerful her magic was. Not only powerful, but ancient. As ancient as mine.

She landed back in the dirt and shook herself. The fur was gone, and a statuesque demigoddess with long, flowing white hair stood in front of me.

Chapter 20

History bites

"Magara! Is that you?" I exclaimed.

Her form wavered, and she turned back into Nimbus. She growled in frustration. "Restrained, I am."

"You've been here all this time?" I staggered back, shocked to see my centuries-old nemesis in front of me.

"With Roland, I have been," Nimbus said. "Trapped, just like you."

My jaw dropped. "Trapped by the goblin?"

Nimbus nodded. "Too powerful he was. Too big of an army to defeat alone. If we'd been together, we could have brought him down. Instead, I became this thing. My form disgusts me. Humbled into being this snivelling fool's familiar. The shame."

Roland stared at Nimbus. "What... what are you?"

Nimbus lashed out with a clawed foot, almost taking off Roland's nose. "Hateful little man. Tedious fungi freak."

"You had no problem with exploiting that fungi," I said. "I should have recognized your signature chaos. This is always how you operate."

"Just getting started, I am." Nimbus snickered. "Once I'm free for good. Almost there."

"You're... not my familiar?" Roland trembled in the dirt. "How is this happening? How is a goblin involved? I don't understand."

"Roland, stay still and make no sudden movements," I cautioned. "Nimbus isn't what she appears to be. Her magic is deadly and old."

"I saw her change into an otherworldly being. Didn't I?" He curled into a ball, his wide eyes fixed on Nimbus.

"She's a demigoddess," I said. "Immensely powerful, but also immensely unstable. And not to be trusted."

"And you know her?"

"Our paths have crossed many times, and the outcome is rarely good." Magara was one of the few demigoddesses who'd come close to defeating me and taking over my many realms.

"Have I never had a familiar?" Roland asked. "Nimbus, I thought we were happy together."

"Convenience, you were," Nimbus said on a hiss. "A trusting little man no one would suspect. Well, no one but Juno. Always had a knack for finding the truth, she did. One of the many things I hated about her."

"Almost as intensely as I hated your love for destruction. You ruin things for fun. There was never any purpose behind your malice," I said.

"To win it all is my purpose," Nimbus said. "Can never have enough."

"That's called greed," I said. "It's a terrible character trait. And it's not the first time I've told you that. You don't learn."

Nimbus hissed again, and her form altered for a brief second before she was forced back into the strange sinewy creature she'd been changed into. "Bored here, you must be. Tiny town full of tiny people."

"I'm never bored. I have everything I desire here," I said.

"Lies you tell. Your greed is almost as great as mine. You ruled many and dominated more. Your power was once so great. What went wrong?"

"I... I don't understand," Roland said. "You're bonded to Zandra Crypt. That means you're both powerful, but what is Nimbus talking about? You used to rule?"

"Nimbus, or Magara, as I know her as, is confused," I said. "It's most likely she's tainted herself with the toxic fungi she's been using on everybody else."

"I still can't believe this is happening." Roland gulped several times. "It's been Nimbus doing so much harm? She's killed people?"

"Ignore him. Too small to bother with," Nimbus said. "Join with me. Juno, together, we can be amazing."

I twitched in anger. "We're enemies!"

"Join forces and defeat the goblin, we will. Both get what we want. Enemies. Friends. Neutral. We desire the same thing. The goblin dead and all we lost back under our control. Don't tell me you haven't pined for such a dream."

A brief flash of hope surged inside me. I knew only too well how the true Magara behaved. She'd go to any lengths to get the power she desired. She must have been attempting to get her hands on something she shouldn't when the goblin caught her. Together, we could defeat him and destroy any uprisings his followers attempted. I would get back everything. It was something I yearned for.

"Tempted, I see you are," Nimbus said. "Co-rulers we could be. No one would defeat us. Immortal and all-powerful. Do what we like, we could."

I shook away the temptation with a flick of my tail. "I know your kind of rule and the power you crave. That's why you targeted Crimson Cove. The people here aren't small, and their magic is mighty. This town draws the unusually powerful—vampires, witches, tea leaf readers—and you wanted a taste of that power. You're building back your defenses."

Magara flashed back into view before disappearing again under Nimbus's fluff. "No option, I had. Desperate when I met Roland. Formed a bond and made plans. The fungus was a welcome bonus."

"You used me!" Roland spluttered. "I've taken such great care of you. I love you."

"Silence, little man," Nimbus said. "Have no need for you now. Not when Juno joins me."

"I'd never join with someone I don't trust," I said.

"No trust needed, just boundaries and respect."

"Roland, you really didn't know Nimbus was something different?" I asked him.

"No! I... I worried about her sometimes, though. She's been disappearing a lot lately but would never tell me where she went. And I keep waking and not realizing I fell asleep. And I've been so tired. I thought it was stress, but maybe not. Did you do that to me, Nimbus?"

"Stop speaking or I'll destroy you," Nimbus said. "You were nothing to me. I have no interest in you. Worthless. Sad."

"Don't be unkind," I said. "Roland took you in when no one else would. You manipulated him, so you had a safe home to make your cruel plans."

"The fungus made my skin crawl." Nimbus spat on the ground. "But then I realized the fun I could have with it, so I played games."

"You messed with people's lives. People have died. That is your fault." I sparked a spell on my paws.

"Do nothing foolish, Juno. Regret it, you will." Nimbus crouched and snarled at me.

"Back at you."

Nimbus roared as she unleashed a torrent of raw magic, her form shifting and expanding, becoming more monstrous with every passing second. I barely had time to cast a protective shield before she struck, sending shockwaves through the barrier.

My heart pounded as I retaliated, hurling bolts of searing energy at her. They exploded against her, sending up clouds of dust and smoke, but Nimbus barely flinched. She surged forward, claws raking the air, leaving trails of shimmering power in her wake.

I leaped to the side, avoiding her strike, and countered with a blast of concentrated energy. The force of my magic pushed her back, but only for a second. Nimbus roared again, the sound vibrating through my bones, and retaliated with a spell that splintered the ground by my paws, sending chunks of earth flying.

Nimbus advanced relentlessly, her eyes glowing with a malevolent light. She was stronger than I remembered, her magic darker and more chaotic. Each spell she cast seemed warped.

I drew from the deepest well of my power, the old, deadly magic I rarely revealed, and sent a barrage of elemental magic at her: fire, ice, lightning—all merging into a storm of destruction. Nimbus snarled as she was enveloped in the maelstrom, her form flickering between furred creature and tormented demigoddess.

For a moment, I had the upper paw. But with a growl of fury, Nimbus broke free from the storm, her body surrounded by a dark aura that absorbed my attacks. She charged at me with terrifying speed, her claws extended.

I barely raised a fresh barrier in time. Her impact shattered it, sending me sprawling. Pain shot through my paws, but I forced myself to stand, summoning more power, forming a whip of pure energy, lashing out at her. It wrapped around Nimbus's head, crackling with intensity.

Nimbus screeched and yanked, trying to pull me off balance. I gritted my teeth and held on, channeling more energy. She stumbled, but then her eyes narrowed, and she sent a wave of darkness up the whip. It traveled toward me like a scaled serpent, and I had to let go to avoid being consumed.

The darkness dissipated, and Nimbus lunged for my throat. If I wasn't joining her once she'd gotten free from her furry form, she'd destroy me. I ducked and countered with a blast of kinetic force, sending her crashing into the house. Nimbus pushed herself up immediately, eyes blazing with rage.

She slammed her head into the dirt, and the ground split open, dark tendrils of magic erupting and wrapping around my paws. I struggled, trying to free myself, but the tendrils tightened, pulling me down.

I cast a spell that sent a shockwave through the dirt, breaking the tendrils' grip. As I regained my footing, Nimbus was already upon me, her claws slashing through the air. I raised a paw, and a jolt of pain tore through me as Nimbus made contact.

Ignoring the injury, I retaliated with a blast of energy aimed at her soft underbelly. She doubled over, but then grabbed my tail with a vice-like grip.

Summoning every bit of remaining power, I unleashed it in a desperate explosion of light and force. The blast sent us flying, the landscape torn apart by the sheer intensity of the magic.

I landed hard, the breath knocked out of me. As I struggled to rise, I saw Nimbus lying in a crater of her own making, her body flickering between forms.

A voice called out my name, and my head whipped up. "Zandra?"

The distraction cost me dearly as Nimbus pounced and bit me, pinning me to the ground with her needle teeth and vicious claws.

"Give up, and I'll send you to your witch," she hissed in my face, her hot breath revolting. "I know where Zandra is. I gave her the perfect dose of fungi to distract her from you. She lost interest in your bond and wanted new adventures. But I can reverse that magic. She'd be almost back to normal. She'll love you again."

"I knew Zandra would never leave me," I spat back. "Your deviant magic messed with her head."

"Easier than I thought it would be," Nimbus said. "Not such a powerful witch, after all. Her magic is muddled with weakness and uncertainty. You're better than that. One final chance to join me, and you can have it all, including your pathetic witch, despite her weaknesses."

I looked around frantically. I'd heard Zandra's voice, but I couldn't see her.

"Keep her from you until I'm ready, I will," Nimbus said. "Never see her again if I decide not to let you. Make the right choice. Join me and get all you desire."

"You lie! You won't ever be content to rule with me," I said. "You'd want all the power and glory. You'd never share. And if I turned my back for a second, you'd stab me with a tainted wand."

Nimbus growled a laugh. "Know me too well, you do. A deal we will make. Give me Crimson Cove and its magic, and Zandra is yours."

I had to get Zandra back, but there was no deal to be made with this furry nightmare.

Nimbus sensed my resolution not to bend. On a growl, she blasted out a spell over my head, and a vortex opened. A few seconds later, Zandra staggered through, a befuddled mess. She was clasping something. My magic stones.

I kicked Nimbus away, ignoring the tear of fangs on flesh, and raced toward Zandra, joyful glee making my toe beans tingle and forget my pain. Nimbus's tongue wrapped around my throat and dragged me back. I wildly fired magic, but I couldn't hit Nimbus at this angle.

"Not yet. You can have her, but I want all of this. Crimson Cove is mine."

Zandra staggered from side to side, her eyes glazed. She looked filthy and confused. Anger surged through me, and I twisted and blasted a spell at Nimbus, which she deflected with a toss of her head.

"Your attachment to this witch is your downfall. She makes you clumsy. All of this can end if you make a deal with me. Put your stubborn pride aside and give me what I want."

"You'll never stick to any deal we make." I jammed a paw on her stinking tongue and zapped it, making her recoil. I attempted to dodge around Nimbus, but she blocked me from getting to Zandra.

"True. How about this? Give me what I want, or I'll kill your witch and destroy everyone you love. Left with nothing, you will be. Broken-hearted and alone again. Always alone. So sad. Poor sad, unloved kitty." Nimbus blasted out a spell that struck Zandra, and she yelped and fell to the ground. She didn't try to fight back. What had this monster done to her to make her so weak?

I had to save Zandra, but I needed to stop Nimbus from ruining Crimson Cove. She couldn't have my home or my wonderful witch. I had to beat her.

Nimbus turned and launched a devastating attack on Zandra, streams of magic slamming into her. Zandra fought back, but she was feeble. She'd die if I didn't stop Nimbus. I lunged into the magic, but Nimbus slammed me back with a stinging spell. I rolled away, bruised and hurting, and hit Roland, who had crawled closer to the fight.

"I'm sorry," he whispered. "This is my fault. I didn't know what Nimbus was."

"There's no time for an apology. I have a witch to save and a town to protect." I clambered to my paws. "Zandra! The stones. Smash my stones together!" I had to share my power with my witch. The magic was old, intense, and sometimes unstable, so there was a risk it would harm her, but better that risk than her dead at the hands of this fluffy, deranged monster.

Zandra was crawling in the dirt, still clutching the stones as she dragged herself away in a vain attempt to escape Nimbus and her continual onslaught of destruction. Her hair smoked, and her form shimmered as if she was about to split into a billion tiny atoms and float away forever.

"The stones!" I yelled again. "Smash my stones together. It'll release the magic."

Zandra rolled over and groaned. She didn't have any strength left. I was about to lose her.

Nimbus blasted a spell at me, which I narrowly dodged, forcing me back from Zandra. "Your fault this is. About to die. Say goodbye to your witch."

A stunning arc of magic slammed into Nimbus and sent her flying. Roland was on his feet, his cheeks bulging as he held a bag of dried fungi. An ethereal light blazed from his eyes as the spell poured out of him and into Nimbus.

She screamed in rage as she battled against his power. And what a power! I'd never underestimate how awesome mushrooms were again.

This was my chance. I raced toward Zandra, determined to protect her. As I drew near, I almost recoiled. She smelled stale, and her skin was freezing to the touch. There was no time for a joyful reunion. I snatched two of my stones from her hand, jumped on her back, and slammed them together.

The magic roared out in a blazing hail of light and sparks. It swirled around us, going faster and faster. My ancient magic activated, sparking inside me and drawing from the center of the earth. It whirled in a whistling funnel and, in a dazzling blast, crashed into us.

Zandra jerked beneath my paws, but I held her tight. She would never have experienced anything like this, and all this extra power would take some getting used to. But I'd be by her side, supporting her with every shaky paw step as she learned what demigoddess magic could do for you.

Through the haze of intense magic, Nimbus and Roland still battled. He was holding his own thanks to the huge quantity of enchanted fungi he'd consumed. I hoped it didn't destroy him. Roland was a good man who'd been treated poorly by a conniving, deviant creature who had ice and bitterness as a soul.

The maelstrom slowed as my ancient magic filled us, and the air stilled. Zandra dropped onto her back as I hopped off her.

"Welcome home." I licked her cheek. "How do you feel?"

"Like urgh got dunked in a boiling vat of yuck. It was a dark place. What the heck was that? Where did I go? And where were you?"

"Now's not the time to explain it all. We have a trapped demigoddess who's been hiding inside Nimbus, and she's about to destroy Roland."

"What the what?" Zandra's vision snapped into focus. Her eyes were glowing. "Whoa! I feel super juiced. What was in those stones? Were they your stones? You kept yelling about your magic stones."

"I'll tell you later. Pocket the rest of those stones and keep them safe. We have work to do. Can you stand?"

Zandra stood slowly and wrinkled her nose. "I smell gross. When was the last time I showered?"

"You really smell terrible." I jumped onto her shoulder and nuzzled her ear. "And I couldn't be happier to have your familiar stink back. Let's go obliterate an evil demigoddess and save our friend."

Zandra sucked in a breath and glanced over her shoulder at the vortex still hovering. "I think Vorana is in there. We were both in this odd, swirling darkness."

"We'll get her out. Nimbus first, though. If she's still standing, we won't stand a chance."

Zandra nodded. "I trust you. Let's do this. Wait. Did you say Nimbus is a demigoddess?"

"Yes! You've missed a lot. Nimbus is big trouble, and she's going down." Thrilled to have my wonderful witch back by my side and firing on all cylinders, we combined spells, our bond fiercely burning, and slammed magic into Nimbus. She was already weak from Roland's attack. She howled and complained as our magic swirled around, entrapping her.

Her wild gaze locked onto me. "Juno! Could have had everything, but you chose this bunch of broken misfits and outcasts."

"Always. I'll always choose my misfits. I also choose justice, love, and friendship. This is my home, and I'll protect it forever." Magic blazed out of me and entwined with Zandra's spell in perfect harmony. I should never have doubted my witch could handle this kind of power.

Zandra kept looking over her shoulder. "We really should free Vorana."

"I've got Nimbus under control." Roland hadn't wavered in using his mushroom enhanced magic. "Now I know what she is and all the terrible things she's done, I won't let her go. Save your friend."

Nimbus howled as she was shackled by Roland, finally defeated. "Sorry you'll be, Juno."

"I'm only sorry I didn't figure out who you were sooner."

"This twisted creature is going nowhere," Roland said. "Go!"

Zandra dashed back toward the swirling vortex with me on her shoulder. She pressed a hand to my side. "Once we've got Vorana free, we have a lot of catching up to do."

Indeed, we did. And I wasn't sure where to start.

"I still can't believe we were trapped in some ethereal realm by a sneaky demigoddess." Vorana walked alongside Zandra and me, Sage comfortably nestled in her papoose, with a belly full of delicious food, making air biscuits, and purring like a contented kitten.

"It had me stumped too," Zandra said. "Juno figured it out, though."

I rubbed my head against her leg and then jumped on her shoulder. "Don't I always?" A whole day had passed since Nimbus had dramatically revealed herself as my ancient nemesis, Magara. She'd been behind all the recent troubles in Crimson Cove. Since then, we'd barely slept as we'd worked to put right the town's wrongs, ably helped by Roland, who used his incredible knowledge about the restorative properties of fungi to speed up people's recovery and help anyone suffering from fungi overconsumption.

"Something as bizarre as this could only happen in Crimson Cove." Sorcha walked on our other side, back to her usual cheerful self, and no longer talking about abandoning her café. She'd yet to take back the feral, fire-starting kittens, though. For now, they were staying in our basement, and I was figuring out what to do with them.

"Juno has explained it all to me three times, but I'm still missing something." Zandra held out her hands. There was a faint glow under her skin. "And this magic is something else. I'm used to strong power from working with the Crypt witches, but I've never felt anything like this."

"You may have once," I said. "And it's not so difficult to understand. Those stones held an old magic. I accessed it and gave some to you."

"Old magic from where?" Vorana asked.

Sage lifted her chin and distracted her by demanding a tickle. She winked at me.

I needed a private conversation with Zandra, but now wasn't the right time.

We walked past Voss's pizza parlor, which was closed for repairs. Voss stood outside with an exhausted Roland. He looked strange without Nimbus wrapped around his shoulders. We stopped for a moment to speak to them.

"We're heading over to check on the cleanup at the festival site," I said to Roland.

He stifled a yawn. "I'll join you. We need to make sure there is no troubling fungi left behind. Nimbus created so much tainted fungi. It's lucky no one died from consuming too much."

"There are still plenty of sick people in the hospital," Zandra said.

"But thanks to Roland, they're all safe," I said. Roland had been through a tough time, and it would be awhile before everyone in town forgave him for bonding with Nimbus and letting in so much trouble. But the poor guy wasn't to know what she was. I hadn't, and I'd battled with her for hundreds of years.

"Have you been to see Nimbus?" Vorana asked.

"She's been taken away. Cythera arranged it all." Roland looked off into the distance, a flash of tears in his eyes. "I wanted to say goodbye to her, but Nimbus refused to see me. She blames me for her capture."

"I'm sorry she tricked you," I said. "You were good to her, and she misused your kindness."

His jaw wobbled, and he gulped back tears. "I felt honored to have a familiar. I should have known it was too good to be true. No real familiar would want anything to do with such a loser."

"You're amazing just as you are," I said. "And a loser doesn't help to save a town from destruction."

Voss nodded. "You've not slept since Nimbus was taken in. You've been great at helping everyone."

"It's the least I can do," he whispered. "I must make amends for the chaos caused."

"You're good, Roland," Vorana said. "And there are always unloved critters needing homes. It'll just take you time to find the right one."

He shook his head. "I'll need some time alone before I'm ready to risk that again."

"We'll be here to help you when you are." Vorana gently patted his arm.

"I hope there's no problem here. Loitering is not approved of." Cythera's familiar stern voice drew my attention. She approached the group, still sporting the black wings I'd gifted her.

"We were going to the festival ground to tidy the final loose ends," I said.

"Tidy this loose end!" Cythera flared her wings at me. "I look ridiculous. So do the rest of my angels. And even though I was mildly under the influence of Nimbus's magic, I still remember you did this to us."

"It was no less than you deserved," I said. "You behaved appallingly at the festival. And you left me to solve an entire murder on my own and figure out why everyone was being so strange."

"Your gold star is in the post," Cythera said. "Sort my wings, or I'm putting you behind bars."

I leaned over and gently touched a paw against her wing feathers. They shimmered for a few seconds and then returned to their glorious white gleam. "I'll stop by Angel Force and sort everyone else out tomorrow. Any news on Nimbus?"

"The higher angels have taken her. They're curious about her origins." Cythera furiously pulled at her wings, making sure I hadn't missed a feather. "They may have questions for you, since you seemed so knowledgeable about her. Old friends, I believe?"

"Nothing like that. But I'll be happy to answer their questions if I can," I said. "Whatever you do, make sure they don't let her go. She's dangerous and very powerful."

"We're aware." Cythera glowered at me. "You don't need to tell me how to do my job."

"This past week I have."

Her nostrils flared. It was so good to see her back to her usual grumpily efficient self. "Don't get used to it. Roland, you're with me."

"I... I said I'd help Juno at the festival site."

"If the angels need you, we've got a handle on things," I said.

"We do. Follow me." Cythera clicked her fingers like she was summoning a waiter.

Roland dashed off with her, quivering as she barked orders at him. Yep, Cythera was back to normal and focused on keeping the town safe in the only way she knew how. It was refreshingly normal.

"It feels like we have so much to catch up on," Vorana said. "And Zandra, oh my goodness, you missed your mother's wedding!"

Zandra grimaced. "Yeah. I have a heap of explaining to do."

"Once the angels are convinced Joel and Adrienne are safe to be released, we'll take them for a raw steak dinner and a catch-up," I said. "Maybe treat them to a bucket of deep-fried crispy offal. You can hear all about the wedding, and they'll want to know about your adventures in Nimbus's vortex."

Vorana shuddered. "It's not going on my list of top ten vacation destinations, that's for sure. It was dark, cold, and scary. Zero stars. Not recommended."

We said our goodbyes to Voss and headed toward the festival site. I was thrilled the town was getting back to normal. People were being kind again, and everything was fitting into place.

Zandra lagged behind as the others strode ahead, gossiping about the chaos.

"Is something wrong?" I asked her. "Your new magic isn't troubling you, is it?"

"The new magic feels amazing," Zandra said. "And I'm glad to be back. But we really need to talk about those stones of yours."

I nuzzled her ear. "Once things are settled, I'll tell you everything."

She arched an eyebrow. "I've heard that before."

"Enjoy the magic. We have time."

Zandra drew in a breath then nodded. "I'm just happy to be home with you. It's so good to be in Crimson Cove. I'm never leaving again."

"I'll make sure of that."

The cat's secret was almost out of the bag, and I was scared of what life would be like once my witch knew everything. But know, she must. And when she did, everything would change.

Would that change be a good thing? I guess we'd find that out together.

Also by

Witch Haven: Welcome to Witch Haven, where nothing is what it seems. Meet four fabulous witches as they struggle with their destinies, deal with misfiring magic, murder, and the Magic Council.

Crypt Witches: Meet Tempest Crypt, a witch who swallows demons, and Wiggles, her mini talking hellhound, while you enjoy magical murder and intrigue.

Lorna Shadow: A cozy mystery series set in the fun world of a personal assistant who sees ghosts. Meet Lorna, her ditzy sidekick, Helen, and Flipper, the dog who senses ghosts, as they solve crimes and save the day.

Holly Holmes: An adorable cozy culinary mystery series set in the beautiful village of Audley St. Mary.Each book is full of treats, murder, and twists. Join Holly and Meatball, her clue-hunting dog, as they solve murders and eat cake.

About the author

K.E. O'Connor (Karen) is the author of the adorably fun Lorna Shadow cozy ghost mystery series, the wickedly funny Crypt Witch paranormal mystery series, the Magical Misfits Mysteries featuring a sassy cat with a bundle of twisty puzzles to solve, the slightly darker Witch Haven paranormal mystery series featuring four troubled witches and their wonderful furry (feathered and web-slinging companions), and the whimsical, delicious Holly Holmes cozy culinary mysteries.

Stay in touch with the fun mysteries:

Newsletter:
www.subscribepage.com/cozymysteries
Website: www.keoconnor.com
Facebook: www.facebook.com/keoconnorauthor